"Coulsight, but Minka or her former career. She didn't want it to detract from her primary focus of caring for her baby. "Like I've said before, Cael, I can't get involved. I'm out of all that now."

"I know, but you're going to have to make an exception this time." His firm tone seized her attention. "A man named Perry Hamilton was found behind a bowling alley downtown last night, beaten like you wouldn't believe. He's president of Stags Technology, a rising software company. Anyways, we discovered he has a disgruntled employee, who's suing him for not giving him a promotion. People overheard them arguing the afternoon of the assault."

Minka's fears began to materialize. "Why does this concern me?"

"Because the employee is your brother."

Brother of Interest

by

Karina Bartow

Unde(a)feted Detective Series #2

This is a work of fiction. Names, characters, places, and incidents are either the product of the author's imagination or are used fictitiously, and any resemblance to actual persons living or dead, business establishments, events, or locales, is entirely coincidental.

Brother of Interest

COPYRIGHT © 2022 by Karina Bartow

Cover Art by *Kim Mendoza*

The Wild Rose Press, Inc.
PO Box 708
Adams Basin, NY 14410-0708
Visit us at www.thewildrosepress.com

Publishing History
First Edition, 2022
Trade Paperback ISBN 978-1-5092-3954-2
Digital ISBN 978-1-5092-3955-9

Published in the United States of America

Prologue

Minka Avery bent down to grasp the last of the contents in her desk drawer, unable to believe how much she'd accumulated in her two years as a detective. She'd written her letter of resignation weeks ago and had plenty of opportunity to clean, but she kept procrastinating. She supposed that deep down, she didn't want to hasten the inevitable, even if this was her decision.

As much as she tried to prepare for departure from Orlando PD, she still couldn't shed her gloom over this phase of her life ending. She'd worked so hard for this, and for a long time, she believed nothing could make her give it up, not even motherhood. She always pictured herself being a working mom and didn't plan to sacrifice one dream for another, but her perspective changed after she almost lost her husband, Wes. He'd unwisely pursued the mafia to "help" her close a case, and when they tried to kill him, he had to enter witness protection until the law caught up with them. For those two months while he was gone, their chance to have a family together seemed lost. Now that they had a little one on the way, she didn't want anything to endanger it, including her beloved career.

After Wes returned home, they reassessed the choice she'd already made, and he left it up to her to decide when to quit. She hadn't yet made it to her third trimester and debated working for the next few months before the baby came, but that would serve her pride more than anything else. Since the school where Wes taught rehired him, they could afford for her to resign early and to—hopefully—enjoy more peace for the latter half of her pregnancy than she had for the first. She didn't want to give her heart time to talk her out of what she'd accepted was best for her family.

Cael, her partner and brother-in-law, nodded to the box she was packing. "Do you have everything?"

She placed the final notebook on top of the pile. "I think so."

"What are you going to do with the stash of earrings you kept hidden from Wes in there?"

"Easy. I'm sending it home with you."

He smiled and let out a snort, but the sorrow in his eyes shone through. They'd worked as partners for five years and shared a close friendship. Her leaving the department would change their dynamic, and even if he hadn't discussed it with her, she perceived he concluded it, too.

He carried her belongings out to the car, and she agreed to meet him there once she finished making her goodbyes. She reeled in her emotions as she approached her commanding officer's door, her badge in her hand. Sighing, she put her head down and tucked a lock of hair behind her ear, careful not to disturb her cochlear implant.

When she crossed the threshold, Lieutenant Gus Channing gave her the same somber grin he had for the past week. Though it pained her, it conjured up her appreciation for everything he'd given her. From the day they met, he overlooked her deafness and allowed her to become the dedicated police officer she'd always endeavored to be.

Despite their friendship, he remained professional, standing up to offer her a handshake. "We're going to miss you around here, Detective Avery."

She opened her mouth to reciprocate, but the lump in her throat made her stop short. She swallowed it and concentrated on what she wanted to express. "You gave me an opportunity I'd begun to doubt anybody would extend to me, and I realize what a gamble it was."

"I never considered it like that, but if it was, I hit the jackpot. I'd do it all again without blinking if you gave me the chance."

She ran her finger around her shield while she held it, its familiarity soothing her. "I consider it the greatest honor of my life to have served under you. This department and job have exceeded all of my expectations."

"Well, you've done more than your share to make it that way."

She managed to thank him and dropped her badge onto his desk. The act didn't make much of a sound, but it clashed like cymbals through her soul. When she left the room, her fellow officers rose from their seats and applauded. She'd already given a speech at her going-away party the night before, so she waved and made a quiet exit. Overcome with emotion, she rested her hand on her small baby bump, and a flutter of movement from her child tickled her, reminding her of her reason for doing this.

She stepped into Cael's car for a final ride from the precinct and gazed at the building that meant so much to her. "The end of an adventure," she said on a sigh.

"And the beginning of a new one." He squeezed her hand. "In this family, we're never short on excitement."

Chapter One

Eighteen Months Later

In a heated pursuit, Minka struggled to keep up with her mark. No matter where she strode, the other woman's faster pace kept her ten strides ahead. Minka instructed herself to keep her distance like she would've on any other tail, but when the perpetrator was carrying such valuable goods, she couldn't risk her getting away.

Minka considered her methods, not wanting to end up on the news for using unnecessary force. When she caught up to her suspect at last, she decided to holler, "Ma'am, stop!"

The whole throng of female customers pivoted to study her, making her blush. Her speech impediment, caused by her deafness, often elicited such stares. Overcoming embarrassment, she sprinted up to the young blonde. "I'm sorry, but you have my diaper bag. We were in the same dressing room, and one of us must've picked the wrong one up off the floor."

The woman's wide-set eyes flashed first to Minka, then to the identical bag, and back to Minka. "Oh, man. I'm glad you noticed. I would've been lost without it."

The mothers exchanged bags and wished each other a nice day. Minka retraced her steps back to the store, where she could now pay for her purchases. After she checked out and grabbed her buys, she took her fourteen-month-old daughter, Caela, into the mall's concourse and headed to the food court to meet Wes.

"Why are you sweating? Were the shopping deals all that great?"

"No. Another mother ran off with the baby's diaper bag by mistake."

He rose from the table where he'd been waiting. "Didn't you use to chase hardened felons for a living?"

"Yeah, but never when I was behind a stroller in a crowded shopping mall. It wouldn't have happened, either, if you'd bought me the designer diaper bag I asked for instead of making me carry the same one everybody puts on their registry. It'd stand out."

"Sure, no one would dare swipe a luxury bag."

She gave him a coy grin and stepped aside to let him take over the stroller. In truth, she had grown accustomed to a slower lifestyle since she left the police department. She'd adjusted well to domestic life as a stay-at-home mom, though she missed the thrill of law enforcement now and then.

As they wandered out to the parking lot, she swiped through her phone. She found a missed call from Cael, but he didn't leave a voicemail. She figured it concerned dinner with him and his new girlfriend the next evening, so she started to return it after she'd settled into the passenger's seat of their SUV.

While Wes loaded up Caela and the stroller, her phone began to vibrate. Expecting to see Cael's name, she paused the instant she spotted the unfamiliar number. She hesitated to answer it, given the abundance of telemarketers, but the local area code intrigued her.

"Hello?"

The caller didn't speak, but various noises crackled

in the background.

She almost terminated the call, but her instincts told her not to. "Who is this?"

Heavy breathing rumbled across the line.

"I'll have you know I'm a trained detective."

"That's why I called. I need your help, Minks."

She didn't need further information to realize his identity. "Robin, what's going on?"

"You won't believe me." Her brother's voice sounded weak, like it always did when he was in trouble.

"About what? Tell me."

"Nothing. Sorry I bothered you."

He hung up.

****

Having called Robin back twice, Minka stuffed the phone back into her bag, certain he wouldn't answer. Once he set his mind, no one could change it. She wished he would use that determination to drive him to worthwhile pursuits, rather than wasting money, passing the blame, and avoiding his family, like at present.

During their drive home, she refrained from telling Wes about the call and buried her trembling hands between her crossed legs so he wouldn't notice them. The conversation had shaken her, but the simple fact that he'd called her stunned her even more. They hadn't kept in touch through most of their adult lives, allowing their mom to play their go-between. In the occasional updates she gave Minka, she didn't elaborate past his moves and job changes due to the siblings' strained relationship.

They hadn't suffered a true falling out, but they

took separate paths that never seemed to meet. She didn't agree with some of his bad choices through the years, and he didn't take her criticism well. Nonetheless, she never wanted him to land in serious trouble like she believed he may be facing now.

He must've been up against some dire circumstances to seek her help, which scared her. He'd fallen into the law's bad graces on a few occasions and suffered financial woes but had never once consulted her. What could send him running to her for the first time since childhood?

He said he'd called because she was a detective, convincing her that his dilemma had to involve a crime of some sort. His taunt that she wouldn't believe him didn't disturb or bother her, considering her experience with his deceitful side. Still, his apology for bothering her stung, even if it was an empty way to excuse himself. Of all the thoughts he might have about her, she didn't want him to deem himself unworthy of her attention.

When Wes navigated into the driveway of their home in Ocoee, they found Cael's car. The two questioned each other about his unexpected visit, but because of his habit of dropping by unannounced, it didn't alarm either of them. She opened her door and greeted him, but the cautious glints in his eyes took her aback. She batted away her anxieties, figuring her exchange with Robin had just rattled her nerves.

He smiled and acted like his usual self, telling them he was in the area and decided to wait a few minutes in case they arrived soon. His claim made Minka more suspicious, recognizing it as a statement he used around suspects. She braced herself for what may await her once they ventured inside.

She took the time to put away her finds from the mall, with the brothers chatting and keeping the baby occupied. On her way into the kitchen, she asked if he would like to stay for dinner.

"No, but thanks. Autumn and I have a date, so I'll need to leave soon. Before I do, could I talk to you about a case?"

It complimented her that Cael valued her insight, but Minka tried her best to repress her love for her former career. She didn't want it to detract from her primary focus of caring for her baby. "Like I've said before, Cael, I can't get involved. I'm out of all that now."

"I know, but you're going to have to make an exception this time." His firm tone seized her attention. "A man named Perry Hamilton was found behind a bowling alley downtown last night, beaten like you wouldn't believe. He's president of Stags Technology, a rising software company. Anyways, we discovered he has a disgruntled employee, who's suing him for not giving him a promotion. People overheard them arguing the afternoon of the assault."

Minka's fears began to materialize. "Why does this concern me?"

"Because the employee is your brother."

Wes's eyes widened. "Robin?"

"He's the only one I have, to my disappointment." She tried to fight her personal feelings and address the matter like a detective. "Is Hamilton conscious?"

"No, he's been comatose since the attack."

"Did they find a weapon?" Wes inquired.

"Some scrap metal was laying nearby, but it didn't

have any DNA or prints on it. They suspect the perp took it with him."

"Have you questioned Robin?" Minka's stomach started to churn.

"No, that's the reason I'm here. We've called him and gone to his apartment, but we have yet to track him down. It seems he's on the run."

Wes turned to his wife. "I didn't realize he lived around here."

"It's news to me. Mom always acts like he's up north. He sent a card with her and Dad when they first visited Caela, but Mom signed it for him. That was all he did when Wes 'died,' too." She referred to her husband's faked demise when he had to enter WITSEC.

"He didn't attend my funeral?" Wes seemed insulted.

"He said he was working in New Orleans."

Cael grimaced. "According to what we've found, he's lived just outside Kissimmee for over two years."

"Ouch," Wes replied. "Not all that far away."

Minka didn't let the information hurt her, although it meant her parents had also misled her. "I suppose I should tell you he called me about half an hour ago."

"What'd he say?" Cael asked.

She related the puzzling conversation to them both, taking her phone so she could give him the number he used in hopes they could track it.

He thanked her and asked for another favor. "Would you be able to call your folks tonight to find out if they know anything?"

She gave him a sidelong glance. "Boy, you're just full of good cheer, aren't you?"

****

Continuing to shift her stares from her phone to the clock, Minka couldn't summon the courage to make the call. She loved her parents, but underlying issues made the impending conversation difficult. For one thing, they never concurred on anything with regard to Robin. He'd leaned on them much more than she had, and on several occasions, she voiced her belief that they'd enabled him to remain dependent. Her folks wouldn't hear it and insisted he needed support.

It didn't embitter her, realizing they'd support her if she were down and out, too. They'd proven that when they begged her to relocate closer to them after Wes had gone into protection. Even so, she didn't agree with their shielding him from the consequences of his actions—and vowed not to do that to her own child.

On top of that difference of opinion, their relationship changed after they learned how she'd hidden the truth about Wes's ordeal with the mob from them. His supposed death had devastated them, and they didn't find any humor in the deception once they discovered what really happened. After Minka and Cael detained the mobsters he'd gone after, he was free to return home, but his in-laws didn't join in the celebration. Pained by the betrayal, they didn't even attempt to meet Caela until months after her birth.

For almost a year, Minka expressed how much she'd ached to tell them what was going on. At one point, she managed to convince them withholding it had been for their protection. Soon thereafter, though, they found out that Wes's mom and dad had been in on the secret all along. Needless to say, it worsened their hard feelings.

Seeing the clock tick past nine, she sighed and

clutched her phone, aware of their early bedtime. She mustered the strength to place the call but still almost had to gasp for air the instant her mom greeted her. She recaptured her composure at once, wanting to open their exchange with levity. With her dad, Ed, already asleep, she and her mom, Joyce, chatted about their husbands and Caela, along with a variety of topics in between. They'd repeated the same, shallow chatter time and again over the past year and a half, which left Minka crippled with guilt and emptiness inside. After this conversation, however, she feared an array of other emotions would crowd those out.

Truth be told, she was tempted to let the exchange end as it wound down, but she knew she couldn't. "Have you talked to Robin lately?"

Her mom hesitated, no doubt due to the rarity of her asking about her brother. "Not in the past couple of days, but he was doing well the last time we spoke."

Minka decided not to mention he'd contacted her that afternoon for the moment. "Good. I'm sorry he hasn't met Caela yet. We meant to visit him last summer, but we decided to wait till she grew a little older before we took a long trip. Maybe we can make it this year. Where's he living these days?"

Her mom's reply again teemed with uncertainty. "He's back in Florida. The company he works for transferred him."

"Really? He should've given us a call."

Wes shot her an amused smile.

"Well, he works a lot of hours. He's trying to be promoted, but his boss is giving him a hard time."

Sensing her mother's guard lowering, Minka pursued the matter. "It's a dog-eat-dog world. What company is it?"

"Stags Technology. They make software, but don't ask me what Robin does. He's told me, but I don't understand any of it."

"I doubt I would, either." She inched her way to her destination. "I'd never heard of them until today. Cael's working a case involving their president."

"Oh? What's going on with him?"

"He was attacked the other night behind a bowling alley. With his wallet intact and everything, it doesn't appear to be a mugging."

"Well, I hope they find whoever's responsible."

Despite the sentiment, Minka noted a change in her mom's voice. "Me, too." She paused but reminded herself she couldn't stall any longer. "Before Cael told me about it, Robin called me, Mom. He said he needed my help, but he wouldn't say why. I'm afraid it has something to do with this. I'm not sure if he told you, but he's filed a lawsuit against the victim."

"Because he didn't get promoted. Yes, he shared it with me." Her mother snapped back into protect mode. "There's a big difference between a lawsuit and a brutal assault, Minka."

"I understand that, but you have to admit, one can lead to the other. I'm not saying he's guilty at all, but it looks bad."

"Well, you're just going to have to believe in him, like a sister should."

Her words made Minka flinch, and she couldn't help but notice the similarity to Robin's accusation. "I can do that, but Cael and the police can't."

The reference to her brother-in-law didn't help matters. "Speaking of Cael, what if he were in this predicament? Wouldn't you defend him?"

"Not if the evidence told me otherwise."

"Then, what evidence do you have against Robin?"

Trapped by the same wiliness she'd inherited, Minka debated how to respond. "Look, I'm not trying to throw him in jail. All I need you to tell me is where he's gone."

"I don't know. He just moved a couple months ago, and I haven't asked for his address yet."

She didn't want to fire up a useless argument over her honesty, so Minka appealed to her powers of reason. "Fine, but please convey to him the need to contact us. As long as he has a solid alibi, he doesn't need to hide. He should just tell it to the police, and he can put it behind him. You have to keep in mind how serious this is, Mom. If this goes south and you withhold information, you could be an accessory to murder."

"I understand that, and you, of all people, should understand the cost of protecting someone you love."

As the connection broke, Minka struggled to dab away the tears flowing down her cheeks with quivering hands.

****

Caela didn't cry for her more than once, but Minka didn't sleep well. Her discussion with her mom replayed in her mind all night long, each time giving her a bleaker outlook on life. They'd had their share of arguments, but none with this much at stake. This involved their entire family, not to mention the law.

Being a mother herself, Minka appreciated why her mom wanted to protect Robin and why she'd want her to, as well. He was her brother, and even she wished she could have more faith in him. Because of his past, along with her experience on the force, however, she found it difficult to cut him much slack.

When she rose to begin her Sunday, she didn't hold out any hope for relaxation from the start. A text from Cael awaited her, revealing that the number she gave him had been from a burner phone and had gone off the grid after Robin called her. She agreed with Cael's assumption that he took out the battery, considering his savviness with technology. He didn't have anything further to report, so she firmed up the time for their dinner with him and his girlfriend.

In no mood for company, she wished she could cancel their plans, but she appreciated his desire for them to get better acquainted with Autumn. They hadn't been dating for long, but Minka could tell he was serious about her by the way he talked and acted when he mentioned her. Plus, Minka welcomed the opportunity to get together, given he didn't spend as much time with them since he met her.

Still, she lacked enthusiasm about their evening ahead. Because Autumn ate no meat, she planned to make a vegetarian lasagna for the first time, which made her nervous. She also worried over Autumn's impression of them, considering the fact that Cael and she became connected through an aerobics class he'd taken Caela to. After he met her in passing and learned that she headed up a class for toddlers, he begged Minka to let him enroll Caela.

She'd reluctantly agreed, doubting it would go beyond a couple of sessions. Now that it culminated into a true relationship, she didn't like the message her failure to take her own daughter could send.

All too soon, Cael and Autumn were set to arrive within minutes, and she hustled to set the table. With the football game over, Wes offered to lend a hand, but Caela's cry commanded him over to her playpen. The foul odor that wafted through the living room explained her distress.

Once he finished changing her diaper, he carried the cleaned-up little one into the kitchen as Minka was tossing her salad.

"Somebody smells good." Minka kissed her daughter's tiny hand.

"Thanks, babe." Wes grinned. "I wanted to be fresh to show Autumn who's the more attractive Avery."

She rolled her eyes. "Brothers."

He shrugged. "While we're on that subject, any updates on Robin since this morning?"

"Afraid not."

He set Caela into her highchair. "I still don't buy that he's capable of this. Sure, he's landed in a couple messes with the law before, but I just can't fathom he'd almost kill a guy."

"I haven't been around him enough to determine what I can rule out."

He caressed her shoulder to comfort her and asked again what he could do to help. She designated him to chop onions for the salad so she could fix her disheveled ponytail. Not long after she brushed her auburn locks and put them into a bun, the doorbell rang, and she rushed to Wes's side to greet them.

The couples exchanged salutations before taking a seat in the living room. Minka and Wes had met the bubbly fitness instructor once when they and Cael swapped off Caela at Autumn's studio, but they didn't get much past introductions. They made pleasant small talk, and Autumn impressed her. She spoke with candor and joked around, proving to be much more down-to-earth than Minka expected. Minka also noted the contrast between her appearance inside and outside the gym, as her styled red hair glistened with natural highlights and her flawless complexion glowed when it wasn't saturated by sweat. Overall, she was, in fact, just the type of girl she'd always pictured Cael marrying.

That said, nobody's perfect, and it didn't take her a whole evening to deduce that Autumn was no exception. They hadn't even made it to dessert when the trainer's curiosity veered into the direction Minka would've rather avoided.

"Is there any chance of Caela losing her hearing?" Autumn inquired.

Minka fought her irritation over the blunt curiosity. "Not due to heredity. I'm deaf because I was born almost two months premature."

"I see. How old were you when they put in the cochlear implant?"

"I'd just turned ten."

"That's great."

Autumn took another bite of salad, and Minka hoped she'd learned all she wanted to. She wracked her mind to select another subject to introduce, but she didn't brainstorm fast enough.

"Does Caela understand your speech all right?"

Her indignation rose, but she kept her cool. "She seems to."

"Yeah, she probably has a harder time with my lingo," Wes said.

Autumn grinned but seemed oblivious to the

awkward vibe lingering among them. "Sign language has always interested me. Cael's promised to teach me, but could you show me a few words? You're the pro."

Beside her, Wes tapped her knee under the table and finger-spelled, *Be nice.*

She heeded his counsel, demonstrating how to sign her own name and told Autumn she was beautiful. Once Cael translated what Minka had expressed, Autumn signed back *Thank you*, announcing that she'd learned the phrase in middle school.

In an attempt to end the discussion, Minka stood to serve the French silk pie she'd bought, and Cael rose to assist her. Once the door closed behind him, he was quick to apologize for his date's behavior.

"I'm sorry if Autumn made you uncomfortable with the deaf talk. I think she's a little nervous."

"She doesn't seem to be. It takes quite a bit of nerve to ask if my baby understands me."

"She could use a lesson on tact, but I'm telling you, she didn't mean any harm."

"I'll accept that." A devilish grin crossed her lips. "In fact, I'd love to help you teach her ASL."

"She's not ready for a crash course like that, Minks."

She snickered at the thought of the scenario. While they were alone, she seized the opportunity to ask him about her brother. "Any news on the case?"

He shook his head. "You said your mom didn't indicate anything?"

"Nope, she was too busy scolding me for being a horrible sister. I would've had more success talking to Robin's doormat."

He offered a pat on her back. "Thanks for trying."

As she dished out the last slice of pie, her phone started vibrating in her pocket. Just like yesterday, she found a number she didn't recognize, which made her suspicious. She regarded Cael with the knowing countenance they'd exchanged many times.

Her brother didn't give her the chance to greet him. "Mom says you think I'm some vicious animal. I know my record, but I've been trying to clean up my act. I wouldn't jeopardize that by beating a low-life like Hamilton."

"So the guy you beat up a few years back was worth it, huh?" she fired back.

"I'm serious, Minka, I've changed."

"Yeah, I gather that, judging by your running away and all."

"I figured everybody was going to put the blame on me, including your friends. Besides, didn't Wes run off when he was in trouble?"

"For somebody who's too busy to drive twenty minutes to visit us, you're sure an expert on our lives."

"I'm not doing this. I told you that you wouldn't believe me." Robin hung up on her again.

Minka put down her phone. "What a charmer."

"You digressed," Cael reprimanded.

In sore need of something sweet, she licked the spatula she'd just finished using. "Give me a break."

"Did he give you anything useful?"

"Nothing, except for a phone number."

"I'll have to look it up from home. We'll see how crafty he is."

"Don't hold your breath." She tried to conceal that she was holding her own.

****

19

The next day, Minka dropped off Caela with her mother-in-law, Jaclyn, and headed to the precinct to talk to Cael and Gus, her former commanding officer. She'd only gone a handful of times since leaving the force, so she still had difficulty remembering to park in the visitor's lot. She didn't have an invitation, but she couldn't stay away from the place that always gave her a sense of control.

Pacing into the station with resolve, she motioned for Cael's attention on her way to Gus's office. Reading over a file when she entered, the lieutenant did a double take upon realizing her presence.

"To what do I owe the grimace?"

"For once, it isn't your doing." She returned his playfulness, the two being good friends. "Although I would've appreciated it if another department could've dealt with my wanted brother."

"I'm afraid the cases find me."

Joining them, Cael closed the door behind him. "Hey, Minks. I'm sorry I forgot to text you about the number Robin called from yesterday. It's a payphone in Knoxville, Tennessee."

"He must've either been driving to or from Mom and Dad's." She didn't have trouble picturing her brother fleeing to North Carolina.

"I'll call the departments in the area and have them keep an eye out for him," Gus stated. "If he's smart, he won't stay there for long. Any idea where he'd go next?"

"Not a clue. He inherited my dad's wanderlust ways, so I couldn't attempt to guess where he's lived and who he's added to his freeloading portfolio."

"We may not have his portfolio but checking into

his past residences is a good start. Go ahead, and get on that today, Cael."

She supposed she should leave, but she had to find out more. "How's Hamilton?"

"I talked to his mother earlier, and she said his vitals have improved," Cael informed her. "He's not out of the woods, though."

"Have you found any other possible suspects or motives?"

"He did go through a pretty nasty divorce a few years back, but both his ex and her new husband live in New Mexico," Cael summarized.

"What if they hired it done?"

"Most hired jobs go further than putting the mark in a coma," Gus pointed out.

"Stranger things have happened."

Cael gave her a soft expression, seeming to perceive her hope diminishing. "With big business guys like him, we usually find more to them than meets the eye, so it's hard to predict what may pop up as we dig deeper. We'll keep you updated."

"I appreciate that, but I wish I could do something."

"You can. Go home to your little girl and forget about this garbage," Gus admonished.

"I can agree to the first half of that command."

****

After returning home, Caela took a longer nap than usual, which lent Minka some extra time to disobey Gus's order. In her investigating, she found her brother had lived in Alabama, Georgia, Louisiana, Missouri, and Nebraska—but never anywhere near Knoxville. She took a gander at his social networking profile to glean insight into his friends but couldn't view his posts without making a friend request, which he'd no doubt deny.

While she surfed the web, regret filled Minka over how little she retained of Robin's likes and dislikes. They hadn't enjoyed much of a relationship since she'd left home, but even before that, they'd grown distant. They spent a lot of their childhood engaged in their separate interests, and that gap widened when she started to seek her independence, driving and such. Even so, she hadn't intended to shut him out, the way many older siblings do. If anything, he was the one, in her mind, who'd isolated himself.

Despite their mother's attempts, Robin never learned to sign. True, Minka had her cochlear implant put in when he was six, but his lack of care still hurt her. Speaking may have become her primary means of communication, but sign had always been her first language, and the simplicity of it provided just what she needed to express certain emotions. She could connect with people on a different level and appreciated it when those in her life understood that. She yearned to share that relationship with her brother. Apparently, he didn't.

Minka realized she was digressing, just like she had on the phone. She needed to put her personal feelings aside and employ the objectivity she would've on any other case, despite not being paid for it. After reevaluating the facts, she began to wonder why Robin would stop in Knoxville to call her. She supposed he was gassing up or getting a bite to eat, and she resolved to stick with that theory unless led to believe otherwise.

With both her mind and leads exhausted, she kicked back her feet on the couch...until Caela awoke two minutes later. Thus, she returned to reality and put the investigation as far from her thoughts as possible. She had difficulty doing so, however, when Cael texted her that afternoon, just to ask if Robin had called her again. Desperate for a breakthrough, she contemplated the few facts they had on Robin and how they could net more.

She found herself almost too easily slipping back into her detective's mentality and realized this was the point where she'd be begging the District Attorney's office for a warrant to get into his apartment. Without any true evidence against him, she doubted she could've obtained one and figured Cael would have similar trouble unless he found more with which to incriminate her brother.

Pondering over the tough circumstances, it occurred to her that, in this instance, she may have an advantage in being his sister that she wouldn't have as the lead investigator. Remembering the times she'd asked her family to fetch something she'd forgotten at home, Minka began to formulate a plan to stage such a scenario in his behalf. Lacking a key, she questioned if his landlord would be willing to hand one over, even if she was a blood relative. She browsed the Internet for details on his apartment complex, and a picture of the run-down property exposed the management's unremarkable business practices. She opted to take a chance on their ethics.

To her delight, Wes ended his shift early on Mondays, with no class during his last period at the deaf school where he taught biology. Under the guise of going to a dentist appointment, she left him and Caela, with her GPS set for Robin's current address. During the entire drive, her mind pondered the numerous ways this could go sideways and land her with a charge for trespassing. Even if she managed to coerce the landlord into giving her access to his place, what if Robin had a roommate who caught her? Given the people he gravitated toward, she doubted she could convince a friend of his to cover up her unannounced visit.

Minka almost abandoned her scheme as she passed every exit along her trek, especially due to the heavy tourist traffic. In the end, she arrived at her intended destination and released a cleansing breath before she opened her SUV's door to follow the sidewalk to the complex's office. The whole while, she rehearsed the ruse she planned to set in motion, but she never quite aced it like she did with the landlady.

"Excuse me, but my brother lives in this building and asked me to take care of his cat while he's away, but I forgot the keys at home. Since I live half an hour away, I was hoping you could let me into his apartment? It's 17A."

"17A has a cat?" The woman's cry alarmed Minka, who didn't want to be the cause of his eviction. "I don't know if I feel worse for it or my carpet."

Unsure of what the reaction meant, Minka followed her to the desired hall and gaped when she unlocked the door. She didn't let her enthusiasm show, in an effort to maintain her cover of performing a menial task. Once she stepped inside, her suppressed eagerness vanished. Overtaken by the enveloping stench of rotting garbage—among other odors—she struggled not to choke.

"He's cleaned since I was last here," the owner drolly remarked in her New York accent. She motioned toward the piles of clothes and trash strewn across the floor. "Hope the cat has a bell on so you can find it."

She left the room and asked Minka to lock up after she finished. As she stood alone, despair washed over her, the lady's blunt last statement echoing through her frazzled mind. Although she didn't need to worry about finding the imaginary cat, she questioned how she'd uncover anything of use to the investigation.

Nosing around, she couldn't even decide what she wanted to discover. She'd figured that whatever she needed would call out to her instincts, but now, she feared everything on top of it would muffle its cry of desperation. The mental image evoked a smile to cross her face, and she began to relax until she spotted the baseball bat in the corner of the room.

Minka recalled Cael's saying they hadn't found the weapon at the crime scene, and the sight of it shook her. She treaded over to it, and putting on gloves she'd packed to conceal her fingerprints, she picked it up off the cluttered floor. She spun it in her hand to examine it, and it relieved her not to find any visible blood stains, which should've been there considering how badly Hamilton was beaten. Even so, a crack in the wood didn't comfort her, reminding her of Robin's aggressive nature on and off the baseball diamond.

To keep an unbiased mindset, she resisted the thought and peered through another side of the mess. She glanced at his entertainment center and noted his gaming console—a staple in every home he'd had since boyhood—still sat on a shelf, indicating he'd escaped in a hurry. Before long, she caught sight of his laptop, another electronic the device-lover left behind. She tiptoed around the many obstacles that impeded her path and lifted it off the couch. Her conscience pecked her a bit as she opened it, scolding her for how far she'd gone into the realms of trespassing. Already standing in his living quarters, however, she reckoned she'd better take full advantage of the crime she was in the midst of committing.

Reluctant to sit down anywhere, Minka took it into the adjacent kitchen and set it on the counter, ignoring the spill stains around her. She smiled once she learned he didn't have it password protected, but once more, a sting of guilt pierced her for seizing unlimited access to her brother's digital life. She also feared what she might unearth.

To start, she clicked on his most recent browsing history to discern his current mentality. She found that he was last online on Saturday morning, and the list of sites he visited revealed he'd done extensive research on changing one's identity. She sighed and retraced his session, until she was led to a page that confirmed his order of a fake birth certificate and Social Security card.

Both were issued to a Jack Conway of Knoxville, Tennessee.

Shaking her head, Minka now understood why Robin had called from the city; he was making it his new home. Before she could process the development, she noticed another unsettling image in the nearby garbage can. She retrieved it and confirmed it to be a photo of his boss, Perry Hamilton, defaced by what she assumed was his pen.

Chapter Two

On her ride home, Minka grappled with her visit to her brother's apartment, unable to shake the weight of her discoveries. True, she hadn't found anything more dubious than Hamilton's photo and the proof of Robin's fake documents, but it disturbed her, just the same. It told her he had a genuine hatred for his assaulted boss, and he was legitimately on the run.

It didn't help matters that she couldn't divulge any of this to Cael or Gus if she didn't want to be arrested. Even if she could, they couldn't use it against him in a court of law, since she found it during an unwarranted search. She'd understood both facts going into it, but deep inside, she'd hoped her quest would yield some reason to believe Robin was innocent. Instead, it convinced her of his guilt more than ever.

The knowledge of her brother's alias burdened her most of all. Having worked in law enforcement, Minka couldn't, in good conscience, withhold that critical information, given that it could be the key to apprehending him. She couldn't introduce the subject without a preamble of sorts, though, and she ran the risk of revealing her not-so-legal scheme. Considering it while she drove, she stumbled upon a somewhat believable line of reasoning to impart to Cael, which she texted him the minute she arrived home.

—*I doubt Robin's going by his real name anymore.*

*He liked to go by Jack Conway a lot in our games when
we were kids. You may want to check into that. —*

Once she sent off the message, Minka had to grin,
proud of her cunning, and exhaled a breath she didn't
realize she'd been holding. Moments later, she received
a gracious and unsuspecting reply from him, giving her
some peace. Her venture to Robin's apartment
continued to haunt her, but she forced herself to set it
aside for the rest of her night.

Her reprieve ended when her dad's number lit up
on her phone. Sitting beside Wes, she groaned, but her
husband advised her to take it.

"Hey, Dad."

"Hi, baby. How are you?"

"Fine. And you?" She tried not to let her hard
swallow be audible.

"We're all right." His voice faraway, it left her to
wonder to whom "we" was referring. "How are Wes
and Caela?"

"They're doing pretty well. Caela's getting into
everything now, so we have to watch her at all times.
I'll have my hands full keeping her contained when we
have the roof redone this weekend."

"It's about time you replaced that chess board."
Their roof had needed new shingles for a couple of
years, but they couldn't afford it. "Are you hiring
someone to do it?"

"Yes, Gus's father-in-law. The guys are helping, so
he's giving us a reduced rate."

"That's nice. Give everyone our best."

"Will do."

For a moment, she suspected he might end it like
that, but he drew a breath and confronted the real issue.

"Your mom told me about your disagreement, and I wanted to apologize on her behalf."

"No need. I appreciate how this upsets her. It bothers me, too."

"I'm sure. I should also tell you Robin drove up here on Saturday. He stayed the night, but he hasn't returned since."

She didn't want to let on that she and the police had suspected that scenario. "Did he say where he was headed?"

"No, he didn't want us to know. He's very upset, honey."

"With good reason." She showed no sympathy.

"I understand how bad this looks, and I don't blame you guys for having your doubts about him. I had a good talk with him, though, and I honestly believe he's innocent."

"Then, he should have had that same talk with the police instead of leaving town."

"He's just scared."

"Innocent people shouldn't be scared."

"They are when nobody has their back."

His statement, cutting right through her, made her voice break. "What do you want from me, Dad?"

"I want you to give your family the chance and understanding we've always given you."

****

Minka and Robin had spent the whole summer afternoon in the backyard, laughing and playing in the sandbox their father just made for them. Eight-year-old Minka was sculpting her sandcastle, while her four-year-old brother poured one bucketful after another onto his head. Their exhausted mom sat crouched down beside them, lending her assistance as needed.

"Be careful, or you'll get sand in your eyes." She warned her little boy every time, but he just continued to laugh at the notion.

Soon enough, Robin learned the validity of her advice. Minka couldn't hear his cry of agony, but she observed her mom rush to comfort him. Reading their lips, she decoded her offer to get a wet washcloth to dab at his eye. He refused it at first but relented after a moment.

I'll be right back, Minka, *she signed.*

Can I have some more lemonade? *Minka asked.*

She nodded and commanded her to keep an eye on Robin. Minka gave her a thumbs-up but returned to her project. She added another tower to her palace and glanced back at her brother, to find that he wasn't there. She spun around and panicked when she realized he was gone.

Minka couldn't figure if her dad was referring to the abduction and all the assurances they'd given her that it wasn't her fault, but his comment about giving her chances stirred up the memories of that agonizing experience. More than two decades had passed since that awful day, but she still bore the same raw emotions it left in its wake. Though Robin was found at their creepy neighbor's house two days later and didn't have anything more than some bruises, she always realized it had a mental impact on him. He'd never told her what had happened during those horrible hours, but her imaginings haunted her just the same.

Overwhelmed by the past and present alike, she began to sob just like she used to as a child. Wes sat by her, not saying a word. He continued to stroke her back until she was ready to talk. After she regained her composure, she related her father's side of the conversation.

"Your folks seem too level-headed to take you on guilt trips like this. Sure, he's their son, but you're their daughter. They can't blame you for doing your job."

"But that's the thing—it's not my job anymore. In their eyes, I'm no longer responsible for giving the police any leads."

"It's the right thing to do, though. They're the ones who instilled that value in you."

"Good point." His wife resolved to use that reasoning with her parents. Nonetheless, guilt continued to plague her. "I just can't shake the notion that maybe none of this would've happened if I'd tried harder to have a relationship with him."

"You can't blame yourself for someone else's choices, babe."

She acknowledged the truth in his statement but wanted his advice on one other matter. "How should I feel? I mean, should I just go on with my life, or should I spend it grieving for Robin and trying to clear his name?"

Wes took a moment to consider his response. "I want you to enjoy the life you and I've created, but I know you aren't going to get much rest until this is somehow resolved. If you can offer any help at all, I think you owe it to yourself and your family to do so."

It was the input she wanted to hear. Even so, she couldn't ignore the irony of it, given how much trouble it caused when he interfered with her case. "Yeah, because what could go wrong in meddling in an active police investigation?"

He shook his head with a grin. "Must we go there again?"

****

Caela woke up several times through the night, giving her weary mother ample time to reflect on the week's events and her father's words of counsel. Feeding and rocking her baby to sleep, she was again reminded that her parents esteemed Robin with the same devotion she had for Caela at that very moment. From their perspective, they'd cradled him as an infant not so long ago.

The thought conjured up the memory of holding her baby brother for the first time. She was four when her dad escorted her into the hospital room where her mom had given birth earlier that morning. He lifted her onto the bed beside her mom, who gently handed the newborn to his big sister. Minka beamed with pride as she marveled at him, the kind of pride she fostered few times afterward.

In an effort to follow her husband's guidance, Minka tried to go about her routine as usual on Tuesday. She balanced housework with taking care of Caela, not wanting to neglect either responsibility. In the year she'd been a mother, she'd learned the link between the two—the baby created instant messes, and if left unattended, she proceeded to clean them up by trying to eat everything.

Meanwhile, Minka spent her spare moments digging into the case as best she could without the police database at her disposal. She did so unbeknownst to Cael, but she would, of course, inform him if she discovered any legal leads. Nonetheless, she didn't want to be premature to report something, for fear of him putting a stop to her investigation before she had the chance to get started.

Rather than continue to consider the facts as a disgruntled sister, Minka reminded herself to go into it like an unbiased detective. She commenced her research by attempting to find out more about Perry Hamilton's character. The Internet lent much on the esteemed entrepreneur, primarily about his business ventures and charity work. His personal life, on the other hand, didn't net much attention.

Like Cael mentioned, Hamilton's divorce from his wife, Loraine, had been quite ugly and was the only private matter Minka found. According to reports, infidelity was the suspected reason of the split, but neither party confirmed it. In Loraine's filing, she cited the ever-notorious "irreconcilable differences" as her cause for ending their seventeen-year marriage. Three months after the settlement finalized, she remarried an ex-boyfriend from college, giving rise to further speculation that she'd cheated on the CEO.

The soap opera sowed a variety of scenarios in Minka's mind, but none could stand without proof. Hence, she sought more information about Loraine to obtain insight into her life. Not to her surprise, most of the same articles about her divorce appeared on the search engine and little more. It seemed Perry drew more public fanfare, while she stayed out of the spotlight until leaving him.

The one work Loraine had established of her own accord was Lily's Dream, a foundation for research for a rare genetic disorder, Neimann-Pick Disease. The fatal illness, which causes fatty material to build up on organs, had claimed the lives of her younger sister,

Lily, and later a niece, both before their second birthdays. Loraine founded the charity after her niece's death and had remained active for the cause ever since.

The foundation rang a bell in Minka's mind, and after a quick review of her findings, she discovered why. The day prior, she'd stumbled across a brief acknowledgement on the charity's website, thanking Perry for a sizable donation. She revisited the site to refresh her memory and noted three other recognitions of his generosity, which were all posted well after his divorce from Loraine.

The revelation puzzled Minka, causing her to question Hamilton's motives. She supposed exes could overcome their differences for charity, but she doubted the likelihood of that. If Loraine had cheated, why would Perry give money to her organization, when she'd reportedly received a large payout in their settlement? Did the foundation mean that much to him?

Since it wouldn't answer those questions, Minka closed her laptop and was massaging her aching temples when Wes strolled through the door. Setting down his briefcase, he assessed her with a scrutinizing gaze. "How bad was *my* daughter?"

"She was fine." She welcomed him with a kiss. "Hamilton and his ex-wife are the ones giving me trouble."

"You just can't stop, can you?"

"You told me to help out if I can."

"When it concerns your brother's involvement," he clarified.

"That's a dead end for now, so what can I say?"

He chuckled at his wife's undying resilience. "What did you find today, Detective?"

"First, answer me this: If we were divorced, would you still support my work?"

"Support, how? Financially?"

"Yeah."

"Since you're a housewife, wouldn't that just be alimony?"

Minka took the straightforward approach. "Hamilton's made several substantial donations to his ex's charity since their divorce."

He sat beside her and scanned the screen. "So?"

"Doesn't that seem odd to you?"

"Not necessarily. Some divorcees remain on good terms."

"I know," she said and put down the computer.

"Don't give up your search on my account. It's just my opinion, and we can all attest to the fact that I don't excel at detective work. If your instincts tell you this means something, you should listen."

She appreciated his counsel, but before she could express it, Caela's cry resounded through the baby monitor. Wes took his turn to respond, leaving Minka alone again with her laptop. She reopened it with the intent to power it off, but when the Lily's Dream homepage greeted her, she couldn't stop herself. She explored more of its content, before a photo of Loraine at a recent luncheon in Orlando beckoned to her. The date listed below it revealed it took place on January twentieth—the same day her ex-husband was attacked.

****

Minka lunged for her phone to call Cael with her discoveries, but she didn't want to seem obsessed with the case. Thus, she refrained from doing so before she had something more than circumstantial reasoning to go with it. She hated to appear desperate to dethrone Robin from the top of their list of suspects unless she could present solid evidence that would speak for itself.

She continued browsing, but no more glimmers of new evidence jumped out at her. Nonetheless, she couldn't leave the website without exploring every page again. As she had before, she skimmed the contacts, which included Loraine's personal phone number. It enticed her, but she slid her gaze away, realizing Cael should be the one to handle it.

She wasn't a detective anymore, she kept telling herself, and snooping around would lead to nothing but to trouble. She even spoke the words aloud to sound them into her heart and tore her hands from the computer to deepen her conviction. Before she could stop herself, however, she grasped her phone and started dialing.

Following their salutations, Minka began the story she'd formulated seconds earlier. "I was sorry to see that I missed your luncheon in Orlando last week. I attend it every year, but now I have a toddler, and I guess it just slipped my mind. Anyway, I was hoping you could tell me how to get my donation to you."

"That's very kind of you to support us year after year," Loraine commended the lie. "The best way would be to send it to our main office. You can find the address on our website."

"I'll do that. Should I write the check to the foundation?"

"Yes, but make sure to make it out to, 'Loraine Hamilton's Lily's Dream'. We want to avoid any confusion."

Pleased with the answer, Minka grinned. "Not a

problem. That reminds me, are you related to that Perry Hamilton, who was assaulted a few days ago? The story has taken over the news around here."

Loraine hesitated. "No, I'm not."

Minka apologized and wished her a good day before she ended the call. The socialite's untruth perplexed her, and she released a sigh as she gazed into the air, reflecting on it. Her thoughts consumed her so much that her husband's voice startled her.

"Please, tell me you're not going to send money to that gold digger."

"You could hear me from the nursery?"

He kissed the top of her head on his way to the kitchen. "My hearing's sharp enough when my checkbook is discussed."

"I'm sorry, but I needed a cover story. Can you believe she denied being related to Perry?"

"She's not anymore, legally speaking." He returned to the room with a bag of chips. "Who cleaned us out of chips, by the way? I just opened this yesterday and only ate a bowlful. It's almost empty now."

"I haven't touched them." She shrugged, not caring about their snack cupboard at the moment. "If Loraine's set on cutting all ties with Perry, why keep his name on her foundation? She is remarried."

"Rich people like her stick with the name that put them in the public eye. It's just a marketing move."

The assumption made sense, so Minka tried to accept it and put the subject to rest—but only in conversation. Loraine's voice kept ringing through her mind, while she pondered how she would've handled such a question if ever placed in that position. She would've liked to believe she'd acknowledge her marriage to Wes, but she couldn't say for certain. When love grows cold, people change and do things they once deemed unimaginable.

She continued to scrutinize the couple's divorce and the press's take on it. Loraine's denial proved they didn't share a very amicable relationship, but Hamilton had still cared enough about her to donate to the foundation. Could his generosity have stemmed from his remorse? Could he, in fact, have cheated on her, instead of the other way around?

True, her speedy return to the wedding chapel pointed to a lover on the side, but from another angle, what if her devastation drove her back to a man she'd always trusted? In that case, her reluctance to be associated with her ex-husband would be understandable...and so would her desire for revenge.

Itching to run it by Cael, she leapt off the couch, exhilarated, when his name flashed across her phone. She prepared to relate what she'd found, but his news trumped hers. Her short-lived glee shrank as he proceeded to report that Hamilton had awoken, and he was headed to the hospital to get his statement about his attack. While the businessman's unexpected recovery freed Robin of murder charges, it could also provide the most incriminating evidence of all—the victim's naming his attacker. Cael hadn't yet learned if Hamilton remembered the incident, but for justice's sake, he hoped he would.

To her pleasant surprise, Cael agreed to call her from Hamilton's room, where he'd tell the victim he needed to record him for documentation purposes. It wasn't legal to conduct the interview with her listening in, but he obliged her, no doubt to keep her from asking to tag along.

The moments after their conversation passed slower than most in Minka's life. She watched the clock, the minute hand representing justice's slow but steady march to Robin. The phone rang at last, and she answered it in earnest. She tapped the mute button to prevent it from picking up any background noise.

"How are you feeling, Mr. Hamilton?" Cael questioned.

"All right, Detective. Still trying to make sense of what happened." His voice sounded weak, but she could make out his words.

"So are we. I understand this may be difficult, but can you tell me what you remember from the night you were assaulted?"

"I can't recall much. I was just going to the back parking lot, and something struck my head."

"Do you have any idea what kind of object it was or anything?"

"No."

Cael's new partner, Declan, piped up. "Did you face your attacker?"

"I don't think so. He approached me from behind."

"So, you're convinced it was a man?" Declan asked for clarification.

"No, but the blow carried quite a bit of force."

"Do you suspect anyone of wanting to harm you?" Cael's inquiry hardened the pit in Minka's stomach. The lack of a reply calmed her, but she wouldn't admit it to anybody.

Declan persisted. "Can you tell us about your evening before it happened?"

"I'd been bowling with a friend, but it's all a blur. I

can't even say who won."

"Can you tell us your friend's name?"

"Steadman Rissdale."

"Any idea why he wouldn't have called us with this information?" Declan questioned.

"He left before me and flew home to Quebec the next morning. He might not have heard about this."

That concluded the interview, and Cael terminated the call. His inability to name Robin as his attacker relieved Minka, but her anxiety remained since he couldn't point them toward anybody else. It didn't remove her brother from the list of suspects, and as long as Robin continued to evade the authorities, he wasn't going to redeem himself, either.

Almost an hour later, she'd just started dinner when Cael's and Declan's voices drifted in from the living room. She didn't rush to join them and Wes, having no hope that they'd have anything positive to share. Sure enough, their somber eyes penetrated her when she entered the room.

"Hamilton seemed to be doing well, all things considered." She endeavored to take the high road.

Cael nodded. "He gained strength during the short time we were there. After I hung up the phone, he told us something that occurred to him all of a sudden about the night of the assault. He said on his way out, he met up with your brother and that Robin asked to talk with him outside."

She put her head down, despair washing over her. "What a breakthrough."

Her husband wrapped his arm around her. "He doesn't remember whether or not they did, though, right? It doesn't prove anything."

The detectives agreed with him, but she wrote it off as a kind gesture. If she'd been on the case, she would be convinced of his guilt.

She hated to sound desperate, but she had to reveal what she'd learned about Loraine. "By the way, what did you say was the ex-wife's alibi?"

"She lives in New Mexico," Declan replied.

"You did verify she was there that night, didn't you?" She tried not to seem accusatory.

"Of course. Declan called, and her husband vouched for her," Cael explained.

"That was it?"

Declan raised one brow. "Would you have gone much further?"

He and Minka shared a clear thread of jealousy. She figured she threatened him, given he'd been around to witness her bond with Cael from afar before his promotion to detective. For her part, she still struggled with the thought that she'd been replaced.

Cael played mediator, sitting down in the armchair beside him. "Cut to the chase, Minks, and tell us what you know."

Startled by his abruptness, she had to collect her thoughts in order to report her findings. "Okay, so I did some digging into Hamilton's ex and found a picture of her in Orlando the day of the assault."

"Why was she here?" Declan asked.

"For a charity event. There was a luncheon held for her foundation." She returned to the website on her phone and told them the location of the event.

Cael wrinkled his chin. "That's only a few miles from where Hamilton was found."

"I'd say you may want to give her another call."

She resisted the urge to glance to see Declan's reaction.

Her brother-in-law stood. "We'll do that. Email me that photo, if you could."

She nodded. "Oh, and one other thing. Hamilton's donated quite a chunk of change to the charity since the divorce. Wes thinks it's no big deal. I, on the other hand, am intrigued."

Wes threw up his hands. "I told you not to take any stock in my opinion."

Cael ignored his brother. "It certainly isn't typical behavior between exes. How much time have you spent on this, anyhow?"

Wes crossed his arms and gave her a smug grin, clearly satisfied to out her. "She didn't even tell you about her call to Loraine."

Cael shook his head. "Minks…"

****

Cael didn't relate any news about Loraine the next day, so Minka assumed it didn't yield anything. Thus, she instructed herself to proceed with her life as she did before she learned of the case. Though the stint of reemploying her investigative skills had invigorated her, she strived to devote her time and attention to her little girl. She'd loved her time on the force, but it didn't compare to the joys of motherhood.

Before having lunch Thursday, she put Caela in her jogging stroller and took a spin around the neighborhood to give them both some fresh air. The late morning sun shone brightly in the cloudless sky, so she raised the stroller's umbrella. As usual, the quiet ride lulled the tot to sleep with ease, making her the picture of peace behind her tiny sunglasses. Upon hearing her soft snore, Minka drew back the canopy to admire her, which distracted her from her ongoing mission to steer clear of her nosey neighbor.

Camille Paleta was the neighborhood gossip, especially when it pertained to Wes and Minka. From the day they bought the house next door to her and her husband, Minka's deafness and her unlikely career piqued the woman's curiosity. After that wore off, she grew interested in the usual affairs common to young couples, such as having a baby and the like. They'd hoped she'd settle down once they welcomed a little one, but Wes's return from WITSEC—and the "dead"—heightened her fascination with them. They explained the reason for his unusual absence, but she preferred to believe her own notion of them having marital trouble.

"Look who I found!" Camille's voice boomed. She seemed intent on waking the sleeping baby.

Minka glanced down as her daughter's drowsy eyes started to open. "Hello, Mrs. Paleta."

"It's 'Auntie Camille,' remember?" She insisted on the self-assumed title, kneeling down to Caela. "Oh, no! Did I disturb her?"

Along with every hibernating animal in the Northern Hemisphere. Minka cringed at the woman's repulsively sweet baby-talk. "The ride always puts her to sleep."

"Well, my walk does the same to me, too, after I stagger inside. I have to keep myself active, though, considering I'm going on seventy-five."

"You're doing well." Minka hoped flattery would shoo her away.

"I was just about to say the same thing about you. Your baby weight's just about gone."

The young mother weighed five pounds less than she did before becoming pregnant, so the attempted praise didn't thrill her. "Thank you."

"Before you know it, you'll be in prime shape to make Caela a big sister."

Refusing to return to Camille's relentless prying about her fertility, Minka forced a smile and shrugged. "Time will tell."

"Scoop"—as Wes had nicknamed her because of her meddlesome nature—began to make a reply when Minka's cell phone rang in the nick of time. In hopes she'd take the hint to leave, Minka rolled Caela's stroller back with her a few paces. Like a vulture pursuing its prey, Camille stuck around, even bold enough to advance a step or two to close the gap between them. She didn't disguise her desire to feed on whatever gossip the call had to offer.

"Hello?" Minka didn't want to let on that it was Cael.

"Hey, Minks. I hate to bother you, but I need you over here as soon as you can."

"Can I wait until Wes gets home?"

"Gus is leaving before then, and he wants to be here to talk to you. Can Mom babysit Caela?"

"This is her long day at the bank." Her mother-in-law worked as a teller.

"Well, I guess you could bring her along if you need to."

Imagining how fidgety her daughter would become, she gave a reluctant glare over to her neighbor. "I think I can find another sitter."

****

It took Minka over half an hour to get Caela settled

in with her lunch and a few toys at Camille's house, trying all the while to convince herself she was doing the right thing. She never attained the ideal frame of mind, especially since her neighbor kept digging for insight into what was happening. She pictured Scoop trying to teach Caela to talk, if only to find out what she knew. No matter how much the arrangement rankled her, though, the circumstances cornered her into it.

Driving downtown, numerous scenarios of what could await her at the precinct whirled through her mind. Cael's reason for calling her in must relate to the Hamilton case somehow, but she shuddered to fathom the details. She wished it would be something as simple as them asking for her insight into her recent discoveries about Loraine, but she doubted they'd ask her to drive to the station for that. She prepared herself to find her brother there but couldn't predict if he'd be dead or alive. Regardless, butterflies fluttered in her stomach as she exited her car.

Cael stood at the door waiting. He opened it and welcomed her with a gruff tone in his voice. "What took you so long?"

"I had to get Caela over to Camille's and ready for lunch."

"You left her with Scoop? You said you had a sitter, not a self-proclaimed private eye."

"I was boxed into a corner, all right? Let's just get on with whatever I'm here for so I can rescue my baby."

Cael obliged, leading her, as usual, to Gus's office. Along the way, Minka noted that no one occupied the interrogation room, which eliminated the possibility of Robin waiting for her in there. He could've already been in holding or worse, but she chose to remain optimistic.

Upon entering the lieutenant's office, Gus greeted her first, followed by Declan. Gus didn't speak in his regular, confident manner but appeared unsure of how to initiate the conversation. "I'm sorry we couldn't do this over the phone, but we need to show you a new piece of evidence. If you don't recognize it, that's fine, but tell us if you do."

He retrieved a pocket watch encased in a clear plastic bag and held it close for her to examine. He hesitated before flipping it over, but she didn't need to see the initials "RLP"—standing for Robin Lee Parker—to verify who its owner was. After all, she was standing beside him when he received it at his high school graduation from their grandfather, who'd engraved his only grandson's monogram onto his most prized possession.

"How'd you get this?"

The three men exchanged tentative glances before Cael broke it to her. "Someone recovered it from the spot where Hamilton was assaulted."

" 'RIP' would be a more fitting inscription, then." She resorted to humor to mask her true emotions. She took a deep breath. "Yes, it's Robin's."

"Sad to say, we figured that," Gus admitted, his voice kind.

Her fears mounting up again, Minka grasped for hope. "Couldn't it have been planted? I mean, it's been a week since the attack."

"We've considered that possibility and aren't ruling it out," Gus assured her. "On the other hand, it's also possible that we missed it on our first sweep, since it was at four in the morning. Plus, we don't know how long the person who found it held onto it before he gave it to us."

"What's the character's name?"

"Jevon Hinckley," Declan answered without missing a beat. "He doesn't appear to have any relationship with Hamilton, his ex, or even your brother. He just seems to be an honest guy."

"Not too many honest guys stroll in the dark shadows behind bowling alleys. I don't mean to sound like I'm in denial, but speaking of the ex, did any of you follow up with her about her alibi?"

"Yes, I called her," Cael related. "She confessed she was afraid to tell us she was staying in the area that day, but she still had a room full of people to corroborate her claim of being at a business meeting at the time of the assault. I contacted a couple of them for good measure."

"I see."

Gus offered her a soft expression. "This may not be as bad as it seems now. It's just all we have to go on at the moment."

Minka could appreciate the fact and gave no argument. She managed to keep her composure as she thanked them and took her leave, but once out of the parking lot, she allowed tears to fall for her brother and family. She despised that she'd let her wishful thinking overthrow her power of reason, and she regretted wasting her time on trying to clear his name. She should've maintained her initial cynicism, especially since Robin wasn't doing anything to prove his own innocence.

When she arrived at her house, Minka reasoned

that her investigative work accounted for something. The legal system required thorough analysis of all parties involved in criminal activity, and she could sleep well with the assurance that she'd done her part to assist. From a personal standpoint, too, her mind could be at peace. She'd given her brother a chance. From here on out, though, he had to fight this battle.

Inside her car, she retouched her makeup in an attempt to conceal her grief from Scoop's inquisitive eyes. She couldn't drum up a believable cover story, so her steps up the sidewalk were ones filled with frantic strategizing. All said and done, she resolved to put the busybody in her place if needed.

Minka knocked on the door, after which Camille called for her to meet them inside. Upon entering, she followed the sound of her neighbor's cooing into the kitchen. She found her daughter being force-fed broccoli, her most hated vegetable. When she caught sight of the woman who'd deserted her, Caela stared at her, beyond disgruntled, and despite being little, Minka had a hunch she'd get her payback.

"You two seem to have a good time," Minka lied.

"Oh, we had a blast. She and I played with the cats, and then, we sat down for lunch. No problems at all."

Except for the fact that she's allergic to cats.

Minka noted Caela's red nose and eyes. "Did she play with any of her toys?"

"No, she didn't seem interested in them."

Having packed Caela's favorite stuffed animals, Minka deduced she was being challenged by a jealous old woman. "Did she already eat her pears?"

"No offense, dear, but pears are much higher in sugar and don't have as much protein as this does. I just hated depriving such a beautiful baby of the nutrients she needs. Plus, she loves it."

"In a way words can't describe," she murmured, observing her daughter's scowl harden by the second. "Thanks so much for your help."

"Anytime. I hope you resolved your problem. Don't tell me that husband of yours is on the run again." She let out a canned laugh.

"No, he's behaving himself."

They said their goodbyes, and Caela tolerated a kiss from her sitter. Since she didn't want to return for a long while, Minka took everything home in one harrowing trip. Toys kept falling from the tote bag on her shoulder, and Caela fidgeted in her arms, her grimace revealing her unhappy state.

Minka kissed her baby. "Mommy's sorry, sweetie."

****

Once home, Caela couldn't keep her eyes open. Thus, her exhausted mother put her in her own bed, with the intent of joining in her slumber. She lay down beside the little one for a few minutes but soon decided a bubble bath would better relax her.

Minka took the baby monitor with her into the downstairs bathroom, not wanting the running water to awaken Caela. The tub hadn't filled an inch when her cell phone sounded the daunting ringtone she'd recently selected, indicating it was her mom. Though tempted to ignore it for now, she reckoned her relaxing bath wouldn't relieve any of her tension if she could only sit and fear what she had to say.

"Hi, Mom. How are you?"

"I'm fine, honey. How about you?"

Minka hesitated. "I'm okay. I'm getting ready to

take a hot bath."

"Oh, how nice. Caela must be napping?"

"She had a long morning, so she'll be down for a while." She hoped her mother wouldn't ask about their morning quite yet.

"I'll try not to take much of your time so you can enjoy your peace. I just wanted to apologize for the way I acted the last time we talked. I was out of line, and I truly regret some of the things I said."

Minka turned off the faucet in preparation for a lengthy discussion. "It's okay. I understand why you were upset."

"Well, I still shouldn't have taken it out on you." Her mom sounded sincere. "The truth is, as your father told you, Robin showed up here, begging for our protection and trust, and I was trying to sort everything out when you called. Of course, I jump to defend him on instinct, but with all of his past mistakes, I'm almost maxed out on blindly believing him. That said, another part of me wants to."

"I can relate." Minka reflected on her invigoration for the brief moment that she believed her brother was innocent. "Do you have any idea where he is now?"

"No, I don't. I promise."

She hesitated before saying anything further. She didn't want to upset her mother or expose too much of the investigation, but she decided to share the latest. "They had a break in the case, Mom."

"What'd they find?"

"Papa's watch." Her voice cracked. "At the crime scene."

Her mom said nothing while she processed the revelation. "When did this happen?"

"A couple hours ago. Someone just turned it in."

"After all this time? Couldn't they be framing him?" A fan of mysteries, she echoed her daughter's earlier reasoning.

"They haven't ruled it out, but it doesn't seem so at this point."

She sighed. "Do you think he did it?"

"Yesterday, I didn't," she admitted but withheld her reason.

"And today?"

"Today, I don't know."

Chapter Three

After saying goodbye to her distraught mother, Minka finished preparing her bath. As she dabbed her tears, she realized she'd left her robe hanging in the laundry room and stepped out to retrieve it. She stopped in her tracks when she caught Wes standing on the other side of the bathroom door. She consulted the clock, surprised he'd returned home already.

"Did I talk on the phone for that long?"

"No, I knocked off early; Miller's covering for me on study hall duty." He kissed her forehead. "Cael called and told me the news. We both figured you could either use a listening ear or at least someone to take care of Caela while you let out a few primal screams."

A chuckle escaped her lips as she fell into his embrace. "I appreciate that, but neither one would do me much good. All I really need is a new brother."

"I'd offer you mine, but, well, you've met him." Wes made her laugh once more. "I'm sorry, babe."

"So am I."

"Were you talking to your mom?"

"Yeah, she called a little while after we came home. She can't guess where he is, either. I filled her in on the watch, and it broke her heart." Minka drew away from him despite needing his comfort more than ever. "I'd like to soak in the tub for a while before Caela wakes up from her nap."

"Go ahead. I can tend to her if she gets up before you're finished."

"Thanks, honey." She kissed him. As she closed the door, she stopped and pointed her finger at her mischievous husband. "And please, don't wake her before she's ready. Camille already did that once this morning."

He gave her an impish grin. "Go. Enjoy your bath."

She shook her head and resumed her trek to the laundry room for her robe before undressing and sinking into the hot water. Her showers far outweighed her time in the tub nowadays, so every time she could lay her head back and bask in the warmth, she reveled in the novelty of it. For the first few moments, she was able to thrust her cares aside and focus on nothing at all. After much too short of a time, however, the image of her grandfather's pocket watch drifted back into her mind. Of all things, she'd hate for such a precious keepsake to be what sent her brother to prison.

The watch was an heirloom passed on through the generations, but to Minka, it symbolized something more special. Her grandpa hadn't presented it to Robin due to mere tradition but as a remembrance of the memories they shared. When her brother was two, he'd found his papa's accessory lying on an end table, and like many tots would do, he picked it up and hid it behind a set of dressers. Their frantic grandfather spent over a week trying to find it, and once he did, he figured out the identity of the little thief.

From then on, the two made it into a game, and nobody could anticipate where the watch would end up next. Sometimes, Papa would hide it before they even visited him, and he'd laugh the entire time Robin scoured the house for it. It touched them all when Robin opened the box to find it as his gift for graduating. Papa explained he couldn't outsmart such a "sharp cookie" anymore. The sister in her tended to disagree with his reasoning, but the gesture warmed her heart. It became ever more precious when he passed away just four months later.

Now, it lay in a cold bag, waiting once again for Robin to find it. To her sadness, Minka doubted he was searching for it, especially if he determined where he'd lost it. She despised how carelessly he'd treated it in the past, as he'd even talked about selling it once when he needed money. Apart from the first couple of weeks after Papa gave it to him, it lost its value in his eyes, and he clumped it together with the rest of his belongings that he tossed about in the same cluttered fashion he still employed in his apartment. She never imagined he'd even take it with him anywhere in the outside world, other than to a pawn shop.

Reflecting on it all reminded Minka that her brother needed a wake-up call. He'd never appreciated much of anything in life, and maybe this ordeal would make him aware of that. Of course, he may remain the same no matter what, which appeared to be more likely with every passing day he continued to hide from the law. Still, she wished he'd change his ways, and before his time ran out.

****

Minka found herself in need of another stress-relieving bath shortly after she finished soaking, when Cael texted her to announce they'd obtained a search warrant for Robin's apartment. In the minutes that followed, she visualized him and Declan taking the same steps she had earlier in the week. She imagined their reaction to the mess, which evoked a brief smile. Once the humor of it passed, agony struck her, as she pictured them finding the disturbing photo of Hamilton she'd left lying in the trash can.

Her secret expedition continued to taunt her, now more than ever. She doubted anyone could tell she'd gone unless the landlady revealed it, so the notion of being caught didn't concern her. Instead, her decision to leave the evidence behind troubled her most. If she'd taken and destroyed it, she'd risk being accused of aiding and abetting Robin's alleged crime, which would've made a trespassing charge seem like an illegal parking ticket. Besides, it would've robbed her of her peace of mind, even if her meddling was forever concealed. At the same time, she ached at the prospect of facing her mom and dad if the proof she could've hidden led to Robin's conviction.

Cael remained silent on the matter, and Minka didn't blame him. As the case evolved into a more dire state, giving a play-by-play of its developments to the lead suspect's now-civilian sister could cost him dearly. Plus, he'd always protected her from physical and emotional harm, and those mechanisms would no doubt kick in once he studied the disturbing picture. He'd realize how much it would alarm her to learn of it.

In the end, she gathered all she needed to from the evening news, which tagged her brother as a wanted man. After the anchor announced it, she sat still on the couch, consumed by the bleak prospects in store for Robin. Hamilton's statement about crossing paths with him at the bowling alley along with the watch gave them enough to arrest him if he ever showed up, which was only a matter of time. With the police intensifying their search for him, it didn't give him much room for error.

With that in mind, she couldn't stop wavering between two different perspectives—that of a crime fighter and that of a sister. She despised anyone who defied justice and would've worked with vigor to get it had she been on the case. On the other hand, it hurt her to accept her little brother had limited his options to running from the law or being held captive by it. As he'd proven, he was the type to rebel until faced with his last resort, when he'd ultimately place the blame on somebody else.

Minka resigned herself to the fact that her life couldn't return to what it'd been before the case. While she couldn't relinquish her duties as a wife and mother, she couldn't expect this to blow over if she just disregarded it in her mind. Consequences would be dished out for better or worse, so she'd better prepare herself to face them.

She also reasoned she owed it to her mom to show her support, too, so she called her the next day, if only to lend a listening ear. She tried again to prove her devotion to her family, including Robin, but she also expressed her disappointment in his lack of taking responsibility and her desire for him to change. Her mother kept many of her thoughts to herself, but Minka surmised that she agreed.

Saturday provided her with plenty of distractions to keep her mind off the case, with she and Wes having the shingles replaced on the roof of their forty-year-old Cape Cod. Gus's father-in-law, Sal, a professional roofer, arrived early in the morning with his wife,

Tracy, and Wes assisted him with the prep work while they waited for Cael and Gus. The volunteers had helped the couple's finances a great deal, but Minka had a hunch the project's efficiency would take a hit, with all four of them manifesting childlike behavior when they did anything together.

Gus's wife, Lola, accompanied her husband along with their son, Ryan, who was nine months older than Caela. Wanting to please Cael, Minka invited Autumn, too. When she joined them, Minka noticed her quieter, more subdued manner and wondered if Cael had counseled her on her behavior. The ladies endeavored to make her comfortable, including her in their chats, and after the initial unease wore off, the company enjoyed lighthearted banter.

Much needed after such a rough week, Minka relished it, with her frequent laughter making up for all the groaning she'd done. Without trying, Tracy and Sal created the day's most humorous moment, when she—having just complained that Sal never listened to her—asked for the guys' lunch requests.

"What do you want on your sandwich, honey?"

Giving no acknowledgement of his wife's question, Sal continued shingling.

"Honey?"

Nothing.

"Sal?"

At last, she gave up and marched back indoors in haste, where Minka and Lola had been eavesdropping on the hysterical scene. The two tried to conceal their amusement, well aware of her wrath.

"Just put blue cheese and mustard on Sal's. He'll hate it. That'll teach him."

"Maybe he needs hearing aids," Minka suggested.

"He is going on sixty, Mom," Lola added.

"Rest assured, girls, Minka's the only deaf one among us. He hears everything with perfect clarity, except for the sound of my voice."

Lola and Minka exchanged grins and finished preparing lunch, as the sweaty and noisy men filed inside. The group enjoyed a lively but brief meal before the guys resumed their work, leaving quite a mess in their wake. Tracy, Lola, and Autumn took charge of the cleaning, so Minka set out to put Caela and Ryan down for a nap. Right before she started up the stairs, she remarked that both little ones needed a dry diaper, not realizing what the simple statement would evoke from Autumn.

"You guys have them in diapers?" she questioned in a semi-perturbed manner.

"Their bosses don't mind," Minka joked it off.

"Of course not." Autumn let out an uncomfortable giggle. "Most of the moms in my classes are doing elimination communication, where you observe your baby's expressions to discern when they have to go. Then, you put them over the potty when they signal. It's really ingenious, and the kids who do it grow up to be so intelligent."

None of the three mothers gave much of a reply to the unusual suggestion, but the younger ones leveled amused glances at each other. The innuendo that her daughter would have inferior intellect because she wore diapers annoyed Minka, but she released a cleansing breath and let it go in order to give the tots a calm sleeping environment. The hammering and cackles bouncing off the roof disturbed the peace enough.

Despite the noise, it didn't take the babies long to drift off to sleep. Once they'd fallen deep enough into dreamland, she exited the nursery and retreated downstairs, where she met Cael on his way outside after having taken a bathroom break. Neither of them had mentioned the investigation the whole time, but with nobody else around, she couldn't resist.

"Any leads?"

"Well, we requested more information from Stags on Robin's dispute with Hamilton, and they sent us a file on it. Take a peek."

She took his phone from him after he accessed the document. Dated three weeks prior, it highlighted both Robin's reason for filing the suit along with Hamilton's defense for not granting him the promotion, which far outweighed her brother's case. It underscored Robin's poor work ethic through a list of his many failures to perform his duties. Meanwhile, Robin maintained that he deserved the position based on the fact that the company hired him a few months before the coworker who landed the promotion.

"Goofing off while on the job, arriving late four of five days, and oh, nice, stealing from vending machines. Yep, sounds like my brother."

"Just because he's a slacker doesn't mean he did this to Hamilton, but I can imagine his anger at his boss when he read this. Hamilton's secretary claims the office emailed it to him the day before the attack and assumed it started their argument at work."

She didn't say it, but she could picture his fury, too, having witnessed her brother's fits when he received criticism. "Have you confirmed that they were both at the bowling alley?"

"No, we can't get ahold of the owner for surveillance. Declan's called the alley several times, and we've gone over, but we can't track him down. He didn't offer much help the night of the attack, either. We'll just have to keep trying."

The assurance gave Minka a dash of hope, but she tried not to show it. She thanked him for his persistence before allowing him to get back to work. Lola, Tracy, and Autumn emerged from the kitchen, so she did her best to let the ordeal rest and join them in their easygoing spirit like she had all morning. She succeeded for the most part, but she deemed herself a hypocrite, painting a smile on just for show.

Living up to her expectations, the guys' kidding around made what should've been a five-hour job turn into eight. They wrapped up just before sunset, so she and Wes didn't have time to clean up afterward. With everything in disarray the next morning, Wes suggested they go out for breakfast. They hadn't indulged in such a luxury since Caela was born, and Minka appreciated his unspoken desire to get her away from home and her anxieties. As much as she delighted in being with her husband and daughter, however, pancakes and bacon couldn't ease her pain.

"I want another baby."

Wes's declaration came as a shock. "What did you say?"

He flashed her a grin. "I figure that'd jolt you out of your coma."

"I'm sorry. While we're on the subject, though—"

He stopped her in her tracks. "Not until she's out of diapers. We're buying them in bulk as it is."

"Huh? No, not that." She was reminded of

Autumn's endorsement of elimination communication. "I was just wondering, if we had other children, what kind of relationship would you want them to have with one another?"

"I'd want them to be close, of course. Cael's always been my best friend, and I hope our kids would develop the same bond."

Minka ran her fingers through her hair and stared out the window. "So do I."

"Sometimes, it just doesn't work out that way, unfortunately." He offered her his hand from across the table. "I'm sure you tried."

She didn't disagree aloud, but she did in her heart.

Reflecting on the report Cael had shown her, she couldn't figure out how Robin had turned out so differently than she had. Her parents were both industrious workers, and despite their coddling, they'd raised him to be that way. Her mom gave them both chores, and her dad took them on an occasional job with his construction crew. Why hadn't their efforts impacted him like they had her?

She doubted even he could answer that, so she gave up in trying to analyze it. Going home to a messy yard and living room, she had better tasks with which to concern herself. Until Caela's nap, she couldn't help Wes pick up the old shingles scattered about their lawn, so she focused instead on straightening up the interior. She mopped up the dirt the men had tracked in on their boots, put away the dishes, and emptied the trash.

Their trash pickup wasn't until Wednesday, so she took the bag into the garage with the others. As she wandered back inside, a faint rustling stirred from behind her SUV. Her instinct as a cop made her grab the hammer Wes had hung on the wall. She took a cautious step toward the spot. "Who's there?"

The intruder stood, arms raised.

She jerked in disbelief. "Robin?"

****

Wide eyes fixed on the hammer in his sister's hand, Robin said, "Please, don't hurt me."

Minka lowered her improvised weapon and took in the sight before her. Unshaven and clearly unbathed, her brother stood taller than she remembered and appeared to have shed some weight—due in part to his time on the run, no doubt. He no longer sported a crew cut but had grown out his brown hair just long enough to show off his natural curls, their mother's favorite feature on both her children. The fear etched in his eyes, though, touched Minka most of all, as she'd observed it countless times on him in the months after his abduction.

It didn't take long for nostalgia to wane and yield to mounting anger. "What are you doing here?"

"I had nowhere else to go. After I left Mom and Dad's, I wanted to start over with a new life and all, but the phony documents I bought online weren't realistic enough. I realized the cops would catch me sooner or later, unless I hid where no one would suspect me."

He nailed that one, she could admit, but not out loud. "How long have you been here?"

"Since Tuesday. Wes almost caught me yesterday morning when he was getting out his ladder, but I hid under that tarp just in time."

"I'm so relieved." Minka didn't hold back her sarcasm. "Why couldn't you just go to the police from the beginning and spare yourself all this hassle?"

Robin lowered his head before restating what he'd told her on the phone, "I didn't do it."

"Then, you didn't need to run from them."

"But Minka, you know—"

From her playpen in the living room, Caela began to cry, driving Minka to go inside and comfort her. Her brain clouded by a thick haze of indignation, the young mother failed to close the door or even tell her brother if she'd return, which he took to be an invitation inside. As she held Caela in her arms, swaying back and forth, the baby girl uttered one of the few words in her ever-growing vocabulary. "Look."

Minka spun and caught sight of Robin eating a banana. "What do you think you're doing?"

"What? Did you plan to just leave and forget I'm in your garage until I die of starvation?"

"I'm still trying to decide, but I'd rather let the police deal with you."

"Then, at least have the decency to let me wait for them on a couch with some food in me."

She recalled Wes's complaint about their vanishing potato chips and figured out the cause. "You call it 'decency' to take refuge in my garage and raid my snack drawer while I'm not here?"

Infuriated that much more, she shifted Caela to her hip and sauntered across the room to retrieve her phone to call Cael. Along the way, her daughter halted her plans, stretching her little arms out to her uncle. Minka wouldn't concede to her prodding and restrained her, but after the little girl continued to protest, she relented. She reasoned the two deserved a few bonding moments, and it would free up her hands and some of her attention to talk.

With her phone waiting to be dialed, Minka grabbed it and found Cael's number with ease. Just before she placed the call, she gave Robin a momentary glance and couldn't help but do a double take at the scene. She'd never noticed how much her baby resembled him, especially around her forehead. His smile at Caela while he bounced her on one knee also warmed her heart. In that instant, she was introduced to a side of her brother she wished would shine through always, but she feared he wasn't even aware he possessed it.

All too soon, he proved her right, taking an obnoxiously large last bite of the banana, in an effort to keep it away from Caela's grasp. Rolling her eyes, Minka pressed "Send" without any more hesitation.

As she waited for Cael to answer, and fuming over her brother's immaturity, she couldn't resist commenting, "If only you'd protected Papa's watch so well."

He furrowed his brow in confusion, but the deceleration of his chewing revealed he wasn't so clueless.

Minka didn't hold back her accusatory tone, as her call was forwarded to Cael's voicemail. "Someone found it where your boss was assaulted."

"Are you serious?" Robin's befuddlement seemed genuine this time.

Overwhelmed, Minka hung up instead of leaving a message. "Yes, a guy dropped it by the station. Did you even realize you'd lost it?"

"I didn't lose it."

"Then, how could it be at the precinct and not in your pocket?"

"I don't know," he mumbled, just like he did when fibbing throughout his childhood.

"Are you ever going to learn 'I don't know' doesn't cut it?"

Rising from the couch, he handed Caela back to her mother and stomped over to the front door. His feet lost their determination when he hit the threshold, and he froze.

"I sold it. When news broke about Hamilton, I figured people would point the finger at me, but I couldn't afford to go on the run. So, I sold Papa's watch to a guy who collects them. He appraised it for me one time and has begged me for it ever since."

She couldn't even begin to process all the ways his account upset her. "Who is he?"

"I don't know. I only work with him," he answered in all seriousness.

"Exactly," she countered. "If you work with the man, how can you not know his name?"

"He works in the upper crust and doesn't stoop down to any of us in the tech department. He didn't talk to me about anything but the watch."

As much as it exasperated her, she admitted her brother didn't socialize a lot. That in mind, she let it go and tried to find another break. "How'd he pay you?"

"Cash."

"Of course. In other words, you have no proof that you sold it to him?"

"I guess not." He gave a casual shrug.

Mystified by his ignorance, Minka used great restraint to spell out his own actions for him. "Correct me if I get any of this wrong: You were afraid of looking guilty, so you sold the watch to get enough money to run away. A week later, it lands in police custody because somebody claims to have found it at the scene of a crime in which you're the prime suspect."

"He could be lying."

Minka put Caela in her nearby highchair to avoid the baby becoming a victim of collateral damage. "So could you!"

"Why would I lie about this? I knew how angry you'd be with me for selling it."

"Because maybe you did lose it behind that alley."

"No, I didn't. I'm not that stupid."

"It's no less stupid to run from a crime you didn't commit."

He gave no immediate reply but took a moment to reflect. "I'm telling you I sold it after Hamilton was assaulted. Doesn't that prove I didn't lose it on that night?"

She recalled Hamilton's account and formed a question of her own. "First, answer me this: Did you go bowling that night?"

"Yeah."

"Did you notice Hamilton there?"

He paused before nodding. "He arrived as I was leaving."

"Did you talk to him?"

"Not a word."

"Can anybody verify that?"

He dropped his head in disappointment. "No, my buddies took off a few minutes before me."

****

Putting a new trash bag in the can she'd emptied seemingly eons ago, Minka contemplated the past twenty minutes of her life. Her brother had coerced her into letting him take a shower, which, she could testify, he needed. Even so, she reprimanded herself for granting him such a privilege, with him a fugitive. When she should've been giving him a lift to the police station, she was instructing him how to control the temperature of the water.

Why she hadn't turned him in yet, she didn't have a clue. She couldn't attribute it to a lack of anger, although his face had softened her a touch. Her willpower overpowered her sentimentalism, however, as did her sense of duty. Something else weighed on her, but she couldn't yet identify it.

As she peeled potatoes for dinner, Minka pondered her conversation with Robin. She still couldn't decide whether or not to believe his explanation about the watch, nor could she figure how it would help his case, even if proven true. Selling it to flee from a police investigation did little to attest to his innocence, and many would deem it karma at work that it found its way back into the law's hands. Whatever the case, she couldn't shake the suspicion that more than coincidence had caused it to resurface.

Her thoughts drifted back to his claim that he was leaving when Hamilton arrived. If he were telling the truth, it may take this off his back once and for all. Hamilton himself said he was attacked after his evening of bowling, so it'd rule Robin out if he had left an hour or two earlier—unless, of course, he'd waited around for his boss. Surveillance could tell the story, complete with a time stamp, if Cael could ever obtain it.

More confused and overwhelmed than ever, Minka's head pounded. Adding to her stress, her oblivious husband strolled in from outside.

"Hey, sweetie. Great job in here."

Too weary and ashamed to face him, Minka didn't stop peeling the potatoes. "Thanks. Sorry I haven't been able to pitch in out there yet."

"It's fine." The uncertainty in his voice indicated that he shared her distracted mental state. "Do I hear the shower running?"

Minka panicked. "Yeah, Caela's in there."

Wes hesitated for a moment. "So, our fourteen-month-old daughter can now shower herself, using my after-shave and all?"

She hadn't noticed the scent coming from the bathroom until he mentioned it. "You give him an inch; he takes a mile!"

"Who?"

"Robin," she fessed up out of exasperation. "My idiot of a brother, who's been living in our garage for almost a week."

"Tell me you're joking."

"I wish." She kept peeling more potatoes than she needed just to release her frustrations.

"How did he—"

"I didn't ask." She anticipated his curiosities would concern Robin's lack of amenities. "Let's just say I had good reason to let him stay in there for twenty minutes. He managed to sneak in and snatch our chips, but he never attended to his hygiene."

He chuckled at her disgust, which prompted a glare from her. "Have you told Cael?"

She debated her answer but stuck with the plain truth. "Don't ask me why or what my plan is, but no, I haven't. I called him, but when he didn't answer his phone, I lost the nerve."

Wes wrapped his arms around her from behind and planted a soft kiss on her neck. "We'll get through this."

"I'm not so sure he will." She swallowed hard and faced him. "He claims he sold Papa's watch to fund his escape, but he also insists that he's innocent."

"Did you ask if he met Hamilton at the bowling alley?"

"Yes, and he claims they crossed paths on his way out but never exchanged words."

"Do you believe him?"

"I don't know." She rubbed her tired eyes. "I'm at a complete loss. If he's telling the truth, this could clear his name. On the other hand, it could all go up in flames if he's fibbing in the slightest. I mean, he could've been leaving when he asked Hamilton to step outside, and one thing led to another."

"Wouldn't Hamilton have said as much?"

"Not if he didn't remember it. All I can say is I'm scared to have to make the call that sends him to jail...but at the same time, I'm afraid not to."

Wes slid his arms around her. "I'll stand beside you, no matter what you decide."

When the shower faucet squeaked and the water slowed to a drip, they moseyed into the living room. Minka's inner deliberation continued, the phone in her hand now seeming like an undetonated grenade. She kept waiting for Cael to return her call, and she couldn't formulate the words she needed to tell him.

Before long, Robin emerged from the bathroom in the shirt and jeans she'd lent him from Wes's closet.

He slapped Wes on the back. "Hey, bro. Thanks for

letting me borrow your clothes and cologne. I like your tastes."

She hoped her husband would point out that he couldn't borrow cologne, but he didn't. On the contrary, he gave him a hug and expressed that it was good to see him. The chumminess didn't end there, as Robin proceeded to relate the story of how Wes stepped within feet of him the day prior. The two laughed about it, until she leveled a disapproving scowl at Wes, making him stop.

Caela's whimper made Minka realize an hour had elapsed since her regular nap time. She welcomed the excuse to break away from the bizarre visit. As she padded to the nursery, they broke out into another round of chuckles. She rolled her eyes, struck by the realization that she'd married a somewhat more sensible version of her brother.

While she cradled her daughter, she vacillated over how she should handle the situation and what would give her the most peace with her actions either way. She yearned to establish his guilt or innocence in her own mind, but he hadn't presented her with conclusive reason for either. Remembering Cael's statement about Robin's reaction to the report on him, she chose to test him on it and observe his behavior.

When she rejoined him and Wes, she sat quiet at first, not wanting Robin to catch on to her strategy. After Wes ventured outside, she initiated her approach.

"Tell me more about your suit against Perry Hamilton."

"Oh, he's just a jerk. The instant everyone learned the guy who headed my department was resigning, they started to suck up to him. I didn't reckon I needed to, because I had the most experience. But the rich idiot awarded the position to one of the butt-kissers, and I couldn't sit back and applaud the blatant injustice."

"Did he offer a reason for not promoting you?"

"Not until I took it to the union. Then, he slapped me with a four-page report of complaints against me."

"What'd you do about it?"

"Nothing. Nobody would believe me, anyhow."

She called him to task. "Everything in it is a lie?"

"I mean, I've been late on occasion, but I always meet my deadlines."

"And what about the vending machines?" She unmasked her intent, unable to stomach any more of his innocent act.

His mouth dropped open. "You read it?"

"Sure did, and so have the police."

"Man, Minka, way to show your faith in me."

"Where's your faith in me? You sat for five days in my garage, instead of sitting down and explaining to me what really happened."

"I called you to do exactly that, but all you did was antagonize me like you're doing now!"

"I've heard enough of this." Minka stomped up the stairs to her bedroom.

****

Just as Minka stormed off, Wes returned inside. Caela's cry bellowed over the baby monitor, so he hurried to respond to her, leaving Robin by himself. He sat, eyeing the door, and plotted his next move. Between his sister's attitude and the evidence against him, he didn't foresee a positive outcome in his immediate future. Truth be told, he couldn't rationalize any reason to stick around to face the inevitable and feared this may be his last chance to make a break for it. Something deep inside him, however, held him back.

"How is she?" he asked when Wes rounded the corner.

"She's back to sleep already." He sighed. "I just had to tell her Mommy and Daddy were okay, and she was fine."

"What about her uncle?"

Wes offered a modest grin. "The jury's still deliberating on that one."

"Yeah, and I hope Minka isn't on that jury."

"She cares more than you think. This whole thing is tearing her apart."

"She could've fooled me."

"She puts up a tough front, but she's pretty fragile inside. True, she's witnessed you put yourself in some hairy situations, but she's still your sister and hates for you to suffer."

"Why doesn't she believe in me, then?"

"Because you haven't given her much reason to. You ran from the law, when you claim you're not guilty," Wes reminded him, to which he couldn't make a reply. "That said, she still doesn't want to drag you in to the police."

"Really?"

"Would she let you shower and lend you my clothes if she did?"

After letting out a chuckle, Robin began to fear another possibility. "Are you going to out me?"

"No, I'm not."

"Why?" He regretted asking it the second the word leaped off his tongue, scared to give Wes the chance to question himself.

"Because I love my wife, and it'd make her happier if you decided to do what's right on your own."

Chapter Four

Minka snorted after Wes recounted his counsel to Robin later that night. "I'll bet his eyes just glazed over with that dumb look of his."

"No, he seemed to take it seriously."

Minka put the cap on the lotion she'd applied to her legs before climbing into bed. "Maybe, but it didn't motivate him to act. Instead of turning himself in, he took me up on my reluctant offer to eat dinner with us, then watched our TV, and finished it off by sleeping on our couch. I'm starting to think I'm losing my mind."

"No, you're not. You're just being a loving sister."

"A loving sister or an enabler?" She directed her question more to herself than to him. "He's lying down there, by himself, with no one to stop him from taking off again. That goes beyond loving and into the village of complete idiots."

"Honey."

"It's true. I'm treating a wanted fugitive like a delightful houseguest."

"I wouldn't say 'delightful.' "

She gave him a sidelong glance. "You get what I mean. The part that scares me most is that I don't have a plan to end it, either. I wish I could say I'll hand him over to Cael first thing tomorrow morning, but I probably won't. Even if I mustered up the gumption, who's to say he'll be here by then?"

"He stayed in our garage this whole time. Why run now?"

"Because I found him. Who knows what would've happened if I hadn't."

"I doubt even he does."

****

Awake an hour earlier than usual, Minka lingered in bed and could only wonder what the day held in store. Once again, the numerous questions that had been haunting her since she discovered Robin pummeled her brain. It frustrated her to realize she couldn't answer them any better now than she could the day before, but she hoped that would change. Better yet, she hoped she'd dreamed the whole thing and wouldn't even spot a trace of her brother in her house.

Her latter wish seemed to have been granted when she carried Caela down the stairs and found no one on the couch. She glanced toward the bathroom and discerned that it, too, was vacant. She opted to check the kitchen, which held major possibilities.

"Boy?" Caela voiced confusion for them both as they passed by the couch, which had even been stripped of the bed clothes Minka had provided.

They encountered Wes, sitting at the kitchen table and reading the newspaper. "There are my girls."

"Boy?"

"Call me 'Daddy.' "

"She's referring to Robin," Minka pointed out the obvious, not in a humorous mood. "Don't tell me he's skipped town again."

"I'm not sure, but he left a note." He handed her a napkin with her brother's messy handwriting on it.

I'm sorry I put you guys in such an awkward

position. I realize what's right, and for once, I'm going to do it.

****

Robin strode into the precinct and glanced around the room, already regretting his choice. Unlike his sister, he avoided police stations to the best of his ability, which admittedly, didn't always prove to be good enough. In this case, he'd expected to confront this sooner or later, as much as he wanted to convince himself he could flee it. Minka's discovering him had hastened it and robbed him of the little control he had left of his life. Wes's counsel showed him that he still had some say in the matter, so he figured he ought to use it to do the "right thing" of his own accord.

On the few occasions he'd gone into a precinct, he hadn't entered without accompaniment, so he couldn't decide how to handle his introduction. He didn't commit the crime of which he was accused, and he refused to say he was turning himself in for it. All he wanted to do was show his face and convince these people to get off of his back. He'd detected a momentary hint of doubt in Minka's eyes when he spoke to her the previous day, and considering how few times she ever believed him, he deemed that fleeting second an accomplishment. Maybe he could make even more headway with a less biased officer.

That's the reason he hoped to talk to someone other than Cael. He assumed Minka soured her precious brother-in-law's view of him in the years after they served as groomsmen together at her and Wes's wedding. Before he made it to the front desk, however, he peered into the next room and spotted Cael, who caught sight of him at the same instant. The detective slowed his steps and headed in his direction, making him freeze without a command to do so. He twisted his wrists while they were still unrestrained.

He waited for Cael to take out his weapon and handcuffs, reciting his Miranda rights to him. Instead, he extended his empty hand. "Morning, Robin. It's been quite a while."

"Yeah, it has. I just dropped by because I hear you guys have been on the lookout for me." He hadn't planned to phrase it that way, but he liked how it sounded. He managed to ignore the fact that he'd run and treat it as though he was on a casual errand. Nonetheless, he didn't reckon Cael would play along.

"I'm glad you did. Let's go have a seat so we can chat. I was on my way to get a cup of coffee. Would you like one?"

Stunned by his friendliness, he almost forgot to reply. "Sure."

Cael pointed toward his desk and allowed him to go without an escort. He couldn't believe he showed such trust in him, and in truth, his heart prodded him to take advantage of it and make his getaway while he could. He understood, however, that he'd better build on that this time.

He sat down in the chair Cael had instructed him to and refused to lock eyes with anyone. As he fixed his attention on his shaky hands, his first experience talking to the police ran through his mind, along with the memory of when they found him in that basement…

Beaten and bruised from two days of hourly whippings, Robin sat, hands tied, on the dusty basement floor of his own neighbor's house. He stared at Lyle, the man's other captive, lying on the top bunk of the cold bed they'd been sharing. He was nine years old and very skinny, and their kidnapper had just hurt him again. Robin feared his turn awaited him soon.

"I'm scared," he told Lyle.

"I know. I used to be, too, but I'm not anymore. He's meaner when he can tell I'm afraid."

"Will anybody ever find us?"

Just before he gave a response, Lyle peeked out the darkened window at the Parkers' house. "A police car is parked at your house."

"Can we yell for them?"

"No. He'd hear us."

Footsteps stalked down the stairs.

The bearded man grimaced from the doorway. "He'd hear what?"

Lyle winced. "Nothing."

"I'll show you nothing." He threw the boy from the bed to the floor. "I don't trust you two alone anymore. We'll leave the little one down here, and you and I need to go for a drive."

With that, he dragged Lyle by the shirt collar and shoved him up the stairs. Lyle gave Robin one last glance before their captor slammed the door. Moments later, his companion screamed outside, and the brakes squealed as the kidnapper fled with him. Sirens blared from the police car. The vehicle didn't arrive right away, but after what seemed like years, an officer began yelling from upstairs. Robin started to sob and screamed for help, leading the cop to him…

As his mom cradled him, the policemen interviewed him, but he couldn't say much due to his rattled nerves. His parents didn't tell him for years what happened to Lyle despite how many times he entreated them. When he was sixteen, they revealed that the police pursued his abductor in a high-speed chase on the interstate, which ended in him crashing into the median. Neither he nor Lyle survived.

Although countless people had assured him the blame didn't fall on him, Robin struggled with guilt over his being rescued because of Lyle's bravery. He often questioned if he would've done the same if the opportunity presented itself. A day didn't pass without him remembering Lyle, and the possible scenarios that could've saved him.

He couldn't change the tragedy, but he now had the chance to prevent another one. He didn't care about Hamilton, but he had to convince them he wasn't the attacker, so they'd find whoever it was before somebody else was hurt.

****

Without a clue over what her brother's note meant, Minka sped to the station. During the whole drive, she grappled with her fears of fessing up to her brother-in-law. Withholding information in a criminal investigation was a crime in itself, but the consequences it would have on their relationship worried her even more. They shared a mutual trust, and though both had tested it several times, this would be the hardest one to overcome.

The precinct's parking lot held only two cars, besides those belonging to officers, which relieved Minka. The unrushed atmosphere would allow for a composed conversation between the two and might promote Cael's forgiveness. She also hoped Caela's presence would aid her cause. It all sounded promising, until she saw Robin sitting at her brother-in-law's desk.

Robin's mouth dropped open. "Minka? What are you doing here?"

"I didn't know where you snuck off to and wanted to warn Cael you might be fleeing the state again."

"I told you in my note that I was going to do the right thing. Don't you agree this is it?"

"Yes, but I wasn't sure you thought so."

Confusion on his face, Cael intervened. "Hold on, you two. Minks, follow me into the break room."

They made their way to the next room, ironically where they'd first met. Cael stood against the counter, while Minka took a seat. He crossed his arms, which filled her with trepidation.

"So, you've known where he was this entire time?"

Her fury mounted. "Is that what he told you?"

"He never mentioned you until you barged in here. Imagine my surprise when you said he's been leaving you notes."

"He's been huddled in my garage since last Tuesday." Her statement netted her another look of bafflement from him. "And I didn't discover it until yesterday. I called you as soon as I found him, but when you didn't answer…"

"You took matters into your own hands," Cael finished for her. "Isn't that the same thing Wes said, just before WITSEC carted him away?"

Accepting his checkmate, Minka couldn't argue but cut to the chase. "Are you going to arrest me for obstruction of justice or not?"

He took out his cell phone from his pocket and scrolled through his missed calls. "Well, you called me just before one, meaning you found him around that time. Since you didn't knowingly harbor him for a full twenty-four hours, you aren't liable."

"I don't remember that law."

"That's because it doesn't exist." He smirked. "We'll keep this conversation between us, just like the one I had with Robin's landlady, who said his sweet sister was the last one in his place to feed his cat. Were you harboring that, too?"

"You and I both know an animal couldn't live under those conditions." She grazed over the fact that he'd caught her. She stared at her brother through the two-way mirror. "What are your plans for him?"

Cael sighed. "He's maintaining his innocence, but he lacks a solid alibi. Unless he can provide one, we'll have to arrest him."

"Have you checked out the surveillance at the bowling alley? Robin says Hamilton had just arrived when he left."

"He told us the same, but no, we still haven't made contact with the owner."

Mulling over the predicament, Minka recalled the other claim that could lend Robin a second chance. "Did he tell you about the watch?"

"No, not yet."

"The story he told me was that he sold it the day after Hamilton's attack, meaning he didn't lose it at the alley." She chose to omit his reason for selling it.

"That's interesting. He wouldn't happen to have a receipt of the sale, would he?"

"No." Her hope began to dwindle away.

"Does he know the buyer's name?"

"That's a negative, too. It was a coworker of his, so maybe you could ask around."

Her brother-in-law shook his head. "That opens up

the possibility of him coercing someone to do him a favor."

She submitted to his logic, but the words hit her hard and forced her to realize the grim truth. "My little brother's going to jail."

"Not necessarily," Cael encouraged her, at least for a moment. "I could call the DA's office and suggest they offer to put him on house arrest until his trial."

"You think the judge would go for it?" Minka had made the request a few times, but the department always shot it down.

"I think the chances are pretty good, especially if he stays in your house."

Stunned, she couldn't do more than blink. "What?"

He grinned. "Consider it your obstruction of justice sentence."

She gave Caela a pitiful gaze. "Cael, you can't let an alleged violent criminal live in the same house as your baby niece."

"Why not? You did."

****

Unable to sleep much since her brother's kidnapping, Minka ambled down the hall to check on him. She observed him wrestling in his sleep yet again, and the familiar sight conjured up tears in her eyes. The police had rescued him a month ago, but the wounds his abduction left were far from healed. She couldn't step into his dreams or understand all that he'd suffered in those two days he was missing, but she was sure of one thing—it was her fault.

Despite not having experienced his pain, she could relate to his restlessness. The few times she closed her eyes, terrifying images of Robin and his cruel kidnapper flooded her brain. She figured they paled in comparison to his nightmares, but she couldn't fathom the thought.

A psychiatrist was treating both of them and evaluated them for conditions of which Minka didn't even understand. From reading her lips through a cracked door, she gathered her therapist warned her parents that Robin may have Post-Traumatic Stress Disorder, and she, chronic depression. She consulted the dictionary on the terms later, and her findings troubled her.

Just before she left the room, Robin's eyes opened. "What are you doing in here?"

Minka struggled to read his lips in the room illuminated by a dim night light. "I was worried about you."

"I'm fine. Go back to your room."

"What were you dreaming?"

"I don't remember."

Giving up, Minka scampered back to the door, but before closing it behind her, she uttered a vow. "I'll never let anyone hurt you again."

At a loss, Minka left the precinct and headed home. She hadn't talked to Robin on her way out nor did she plan to join him at his arraignment. Rather, she'd enlisted Cael to update her and resolved to allow Robin's fate—and her own—play out however it wished.

Minka refrained from calling her parents until the situation settled down...if it ever would. When she returned home and called Wes to relate Cael's proposition, she wished he would refuse to support the arrangement, but to her disappointment, he agreed without hesitation. Thus, she began to make up a room for Robin in their half-furnished basement, never gladder to have the only house with one in the neighborhood.

Meanwhile, she kept receiving the promised updates from Cael. The first text didn't surprise her, with it announcing her brother's long-awaited arrest. Nothing followed during the three hours he spent in a holding cell, but her brother-in-law soon appealed to her to make an appearance at Robin's arraignment.

"Absolutely not."

"They'll take house detention off the table if you don't show," Cael told her and Wes, who was in on the call, too. "Why would the judge put him in your care if you're not even there to support him?"

"I'm not asking to be his guardian."

"What are you asking for, then? If you honestly don't care what happens to him, I wasted my time negotiating this with the court."

Minka couldn't make a reply, throwing out the ones she would've liked to have said because they sounded purely selfish. She owed it to both Robin and Cael to attend the proceedings, but her stubbornness barred her from admitting it. Without discussion, her husband did it for her.

"She'll be there."

"Wes!"

With gritted teeth, she hit the road ten minutes later. After she dropped Caela off with Jaclyn, she scrambled into the courthouse moments before Robin plodded through the doors, his wrists in handcuffs. She made eye contact with him just once as he entered the room, and he didn't appear any more thrilled to see her than she was him. While his apparent disgust infuriated her, she chuckled inside, anticipating the moment when he'd learn she held the key to any hope he had of relative freedom.

Cael, who'd driven him over, accompanied Minka on the bench behind Robin just in time for the judge to take his position in front of them. Besides the prosecuting attorney and Robin's public defender, the three listened to Judge Broadley's opening remarks on their own. After highlighting the crime of which Robin stood accused, he gave the representative of the District Attorney the chance to state the charge they were seeking.

The attractive blonde lawyer rose. "With Mr. Parker having one battery conviction before, we're charging him with second degree assault, Your Honor."

It was a blow, albeit an expected one, carrying a potential five-year prison sentence. Minka had hoped for a misdemeanor charge but had figured his priors would merit a greater penalty. Still, the words dampened his prospects, causing her to doubt the judge would entertain the idea of house arrest.

Snapping Minka out of her daze, Robin entered his plea, which, to nobody's surprise, was not guilty. With that, Judge Broadley took a moment to decide where Robin would await his trial.

He fixed his gaze on the defendant. "Do I understand correctly, Mr. Parker, that your sister used to work as a police detective for the Orlando P.D.?"

"Yes, she did." Robin's answer trickled out with hesitation.

"In that case, I'm releasing you on your own recognizance, as long as you're under her roof and are wearing an ankle monitor. You cannot leave the house unless given permission by the court. Do you understand these conditions?"

His head jerked in Minka's direction, his dismay evident. "Yes, Your Honor."

****

On the drive home from the courthouse, Minka tried but failed to wrap her mind around the life to which she'd subjected herself. When she sauntered through the door, Wes, the picture of contentment, sat and graded tests like he would on any other day. She figured more tension crackled underneath his cool façade, but he wanted to make her feel at ease and discourage her from complaining. His plan succeeded to a degree, channeling her aggravation from her brother to him.

She wondered when just the three of them would enjoy such tranquility in the house again. She wished she could soak it in and bottle it, but all she could do was brace herself for the approaching storm.

"I keep waiting for a sense of inner peace to wash over me, but my utter dread won't budge."

Wes didn't break from his contented act. "We're doing the right thing."

"Are we? Because it just seems like we're handing him a literal 'Get out of Jail Free' card. I mean, is he really going to learn his lesson if he's in a comfortable room watching television while I'm cooking his meals?"

He winked. "That's what I've been doing for the past six years, and I've learned a lesson or two."

"My case in point."

"You know, no one said you had to cook for him.

The way I see it, if he were on house arrest in his apartment, he'd be cooking for himself."

She considered his line of reasoning for a moment and imagined the scene. "The way I see it, I don't want him exploding my kitchen."

"Then, just smile, and tie on an apron, my love."

Minka frowned at the advice, aware of her own contradiction. She resisted complaining any further and proceeded to put the finishing touches on Robin's living space. Once she finished, she made a brief call to her parents to summarize the past two days' events. They, like she, voiced mixed feelings, but in the end, they expressed their happiness that their children were at least together. They also thanked her and Wes for permitting Robin this chance.

Their conversation was wrapping up when Cael arrived at the house. She was thankful he'd driven his own car, uneager for Camille to notice a squad car park in their driveway. In another effort to conceal the situation from her, Minka requested Cael escort Robin inside through the garage. She directed them to take his luggage, which they'd picked up along the way, down to the basement.

"Can't I just stay on the couch?" Robin greeted in a whine.

"Not with all of this baggage." It didn't take long for her to realize the unintentional pun.

"I didn't ask for this."

Neither did I, she wanted to say. Instead, she led them down the stairs in silence and tried to shake off her brother's lack of gratitude. After the two set down the load on the bed, they trotted out for the last of what he'd packed, and Minka made her way back upstairs.

She started dinner while they carted it in, but soon Cael joined her.

"Are you sure you're okay with this?"

"I was never okay with it. I'm sure of that. I'm beginning to wonder who the real prisoner is here."

He patted her shoulder, staying quiet for a moment, until he reported another disappointment. "I haven't had the chance to tell you with everything going on, but we were able to contact the owner of the bowling alley. As it turns out, they delete their surveillance after a week, so we can't confirm the timing of Robin and Hamilton's interaction."

"It figures." She frowned, disgusted.

"If it becomes too much to handle, just let me know, and I'll take care of it."

"How do you propose to do that? You've already negotiated this with the judge. How could I march back into that courtroom and say, 'Thanks for the offer, but please send him back to jail'?"

Cael didn't reply, but his sad eyes revealed his worry along with a measure of regret. He hugged her and apologized for the whole situation. After that, he programmed Robin's monitoring device and left the four on their own.

With Wes and his brother-in-law discussing the various models of sports cars in the living room, Minka returned to her dinner and switched off her cochlear implant's transmitter to enjoy some silence. Still, she didn't want to be rude, so she flipped it back on once she had finished cooking.

To her surprise, Robin offered to lend a hand when she began to set the table. Wes's wink at him confirmed her suspicions that he must've tried to draw out her brother's generous side. Even so, she forced herself to give him the benefit of the doubt. It proved rather difficult, however, the minute Wes exited the room to change Caela.

"I spent most of the day with Cael, and I have to say, I don't understand why you named your baby after him."

At present, Minka wondered the same thing, since he'd been responsible for getting her into this mess. "Well, he supported me a lot while Wes was in witness protection. As a matter of fact, he almost took a bullet for me when we were up against the mob. Caela and I could've died if it weren't for him."

"Mom told me that. You both overreact so much."

She didn't bother to waste her breath relating the experience to prove her point, but she countered with an argument he couldn't dispute. "He's always been there for me, which is more than I can say for you."

****

Minka repeated her brother's rude comments to Wes in their bedroom that night, still vexed. "He didn't even wait an hour to start insulting us."

"I think you took it too personally."

"You always say that. Is it because I 'overreact'?"

"No." He put down the catalog he'd been browsing. "In this case, I just think the stress of everything has made you more sensitive."

"Can you blame me?"

"No." He remained mild, standing up to embrace her. "But I hope we don't spend all our alone time grumbling about Robin for the duration of this."

She drifted away from him, her scowl speaking volumes.

"But if you need to vent, I understand."

Minka snickered at her husband's quick turnaround, and she nestled her head back into that space between his chin and chest. Though perturbed by his lapse in empathy, she appreciated his advice. The whole ordeal promised to rob her of her sanity, and she couldn't allow it to cripple her marriage, too.

Thus, she made a concerted effort to accept her new situation, keeping in mind that it was temporary. Robin's behavior challenged her resolution, but she learned to ignore his irritating antics. To her gratitude, he spent the majority of the day in the basement, freeing her to proceed with her normal routine.

That Sunday threw another wrench into the ordeal, however. As they did every year, Minka and Wes hosted a Super Bowl party, expecting Wes's folks, Cael and Autumn, along with all of the Channings. The couple almost cancelled it, with Robin prohibited from receiving visitors, but Gus assured them that his restrictions didn't apply to them. To be on the safe side, they agreed to keep him separate from the group.

He didn't take the news well when his sister informed him of the plan. "Are you kidding me? I never miss the Super Bowl."

"Where had you planned to watch it if you'd still been evading the police? We didn't hook the cable up to my car."

He smirked. "I have some tricks."

He continued to protest, and the debate lasted all weekend. On the big night, he didn't object, but once their company started laughing at funny commercials and shouting about good plays, Minka imagined his loneliness. The older floorboards creaked and wouldn't muffle the ruckus very well. Every time a team scored, she glanced over at the basement door and almost took a step forward to give him the update. The principle of it held her back, though, so she simply sipped on her wine cooler.

During halftime, Minka strolled into the kitchen to dish out some more snacks. As she prepared another cheese tray, Gus entered the room. "You're a ball of nerves."

"Yeah, well, I've had better weeks. I'm so divided. I'm angry at him for…well, just about everything, but he's still my little brother. I never signed up to be his warden."

"I understood Cael's intentions, but to tell you the truth, I didn't like the sound of this arrangement."

"I didn't either, but I hated for him to go to jail right away. I'm afraid he'll get his fill of it before this is over."

Gus didn't speculate on Robin's future. "You've fulfilled your duty to him and your folks, so draw some satisfaction from that. Keep your chin up, and don't let him provoke you."

She thanked him for the kind words, and they both rejoined the party. She passed around the cheese tray, to which most of her guests declined, except for Autumn. She still clearly wanted to redeem herself after their awkward dinner conversation two weeks prior, so she wouldn't stop layering Minka with compliments the entire evening.

The hostess reciprocated with gracious replies, but it didn't take long for the sweet talk to take a toll on her nerves. Needless to say, the endless cajoling didn't lift her already rotten mood.

"This brie tastes so delicious." Autumn sliced off more than anyone else had. "I've cut out most dairy, but this is exceptional. You'd never realize it's actually mold."

Perturbed, Minka took the platter back into the kitchen, receiving cautionary looks from Cael, Wes, and Gus. She decided to check on Caela, who'd been asleep in her nursery for an hour, in hopes the always precious sight would brighten her spirits. While the sight evoked a smile to cross her lips for a brief moment, her furrowed brow returned when she descended the stairs and saw Robin peeking around the corner at the television. Upon locking scowls with her, he scurried back down to the basement.

"Is she okay?" Wes asked of their baby girl when Minka entered the room.

"Sound asleep."

"Does she like lullabies?" Autumn wanted to know.

"Yes, she's just like her uncle." Minka's statement invoked a look of terror on her brother-in-law's face. A mischievous grin spread over her face. "I just hope she outgrows them before he did. Jaclyn told me he begged her to sing to him till he was fourteen."

"Mom!"

"Minka!" her betrayed mother-in-law cried.

He faced Autumn, his movements tense. "I had the flu."

With a smitten glimmer in her eye, Autumn kissed him. "Just when I thought I couldn't love you more."

Checkmate, Cael signed at his sister-in-law in triumph.

Sitting beside her, Wes shrugged with a smirk,

seeming to admire both her bravery and the insight into his brother's childhood.

Minka's mood still worsened, especially when footsteps began to thump up and down the basement stairs. She told herself Robin didn't violate any rules by sneaking a glimpse of the game here and there, but as his steps lost their subtlety, his visits riled her thin nerves. Instead of giving rise to her bubbling anger, she took advantage of the transmitter in her ear again, spinning the volume all the way down.

Unfortunately, no one else could take similar action. They didn't seem to pick up on it as quickly as Minka did, but by the fourth quarter, everybody wore annoyed grimaces due to Robin's recurrent check-ins. In blissful silence, she studied them in amusement while they fidgeted in their seats and could only wait for one of them to break.

Though he'd advised her not to let Robin irk her, it was Gus who ran out of patience the soonest, darting a glare over at him. "Will you sit down and stay put?"

"But I thought I wasn't allowed…"

"I issued the order for you to stay downstairs, and now, I'm officially retracting it."

Having clicked on her transmitter at the start of Gus's tirade, Minka struggled to suppress her chuckles. The group zipped their mouths in the moments thereafter, until her brother caved into temptation.

"Can I have some of that cheese?"

Chapter Five

Life settled down after the weekend, and the four
of them fell into a routine of sorts. True, nobody would
nominate them to win a Family of the Year award, but
they all buckled down for the long haul. Both Minka's
and Robin's snippy remarks abated, creating a more
peaceful environment.

Minka spent much of her limited free time
pondering the investigation. Her brother's arrest had all
but closed the case on the police's end, and though Cael
assured her they'd remain vigilant if anything arose, his
other cases would seize most of his time. Thus, if
anything was buried out there that could prove Robin's
alibi true, she needed to unearth it on her own.

With so many holes in it, however, she couldn't
even decide where to start. She couldn't find everyone
who visited the bowling alley the infamous night to
determine what they might've noticed. Thus, until the
optimum plan occurred to her, she resigned herself to
proceed with her day-to-day life.

An unexpected source revived her intrigue. While
Cael and Caela were at aerobics Tuesday, Minka was
watching television, and Robin passed through to use
the bathroom. She kept quiet on his way in, but her
conscience prodded her to acknowledge him, at least,
before he retreated downstairs.

"Do you need any extra blankets for your bed to

get through this cold snap?" She used the low-fifties temperatures to her advantage.

"I'm good. A basement's a basement."

His ungraciousness never ceased to annoy her, but she persisted in her efforts. "I wish the circumstances didn't box you in like this."

"You're telling me." He didn't disagree for a change. "I know I filed a suit against the guy, but I never fought with him, unlike Josie Walton."

"Who's she?"

"Our public relations executive until last month. I never overheard them myself, but they argued nonstop, according to the office grapevine. At the same time, rumor also had it they were 'making up' after work."

His sister didn't dare to ask him to elaborate on the latter, remembering how colored his sense of humor could be. Even so, she craved more insight into the woman's role. "Did she quit?"

"No, he fired her. He didn't share it with anyone until he introduced her replacement at the beginning of the year."

Minka considered the information for a moment, which proved to be too long when Robin started trotting back down the steps. Before he made it to the fourth one, she took a longshot. "You didn't happen to notice her at the bowling alley with him, did you?"

"I've only run into her once or twice, so I couldn't say, but there was a lady with him."

She wished he would've related the account sooner but reckoned it might not have made a difference. Like many with his job description, Hamilton's business dealings no doubt cost him friends at times, and Josie Walton could've clashed with him over matters like that. If they'd developed more than a professional relationship and had a date at the bowling alley, however, that put her into another category—suspects.

Once again, her fingers danced across the keyboard, trying to dig up all she could on the PR woman. Thankfully, her public position allowed Minka to access a fair amount, with her social media profiles open to anyone's eyes. Minka's attention zeroed in on her relationship status, which proclaimed the ever common, "It's Complicated." She also noted that Josie had already found employment from a rising restaurant chain, and judging by the ads she'd posted to her feed, it didn't appear she was wasting any time mourning her departure from Stags.

With regard to her personal life, though, the posts conveyed a despondent outlook. Hamilton didn't grace the page, but Josie shared plenty of romantic quotes. In her eight-year-long social media presence, the quotations and poems she'd posted varied from the wonders of love to the miseries of it, indicating on-again, off-again relationships. Minka grew tired of them, but one in particular stuck out, especially when she observed that Josie published it the day her alleged lover wound up in a coma.

"The love of a half-dead heart will keep you half alive."

She found the words somewhat puzzling, but she had to wonder if Josie was alluding to Hamilton's soon-to-be half-dead heart…and if it would become that way by her own design.

****

Minka spent the rest of the evening mulling over her discoveries. She failed to spot any evidence of

Hamilton being involved with Josie, nor any indication that she'd accompanied him bowling. Hence, she decided to keep her suspicions to herself, again hating to paint herself desperate by voicing wild speculations. When Cael returned with Caela, she mentioned Robin's recalling that a woman was with Hamilton at the alley and added nothing more.

He agreed to investigate it, but she couldn't drop the matter there. In her research, she learned Josie met with a book club at the library every Wednesday. With it located not far from their neighborhood, Minka itched to join that week's meeting, even if it meant she had to cram the selected book in less than twenty-four hours. She downloaded the e-book version of the renaissance romance novel after she tucked Caela in her crib, and since it was a simple read, she finished the epilogue before needing to get the little one up for breakfast the next day.

Wes observed her reading over her cereal. "You've never been this captivated by a book before."

"I'm not." She set down her tablet. "I'd rather gouge out my eyeballs with tongs than read this. These women act like they can't blink without a man around."

"Hey, it's nice to be appreciated. Maybe it'll remind you of what it's like to show your man some romance."

"Touché, me lord." She curtsied, then carried her bowl to the dishwasher.

"If you hate it so much, why are you reading it?"

"For my book club."

"When did you join a book club?"

His wife had hoped for one of those instances when he was paying partial attention and would accept the little he heard. When he proved her wrong, she admitted the truth. "Last night. Robin told me yesterday that Hamilton was allegedly dating an employee, who he fired a couple of months ago. I did some digging on her and found out she was in one, so I'd like to go to their meeting tonight."

"Like any good stalker would do."

Minka giggled, before she asked if he minded having Caela alone again. He assured her he didn't, giving her the whole day to focus on her strategy.

Contrary to the criticism she expressed to her husband, she praised the story up and down when she chatted with the group, which won her favor. That didn't matter to her, though, since Josie hadn't arrived by the time the meeting began. Needless to say, she released a sigh of relief when the woman she recognized entered the room a few minutes later.

She analyzed her from afar, employing her profiling skills. Josie didn't let much show while her friends discussed their views on the plot, but once she took her turn, she didn't make it hard to read her.

"I loved how vividly the author conveyed the heartache of enduring an unrequited love." The comment reminded Minka of the quotes she'd posted online. "I could feel Francine's pain over Theodore's constant attention to his job and other women. I admired the way she overcame it, especially considering how important marriage was back then. I just…"

She trailed off, overcome by emotion, and her audience applauded. Minka cringed at the soupiness of it, but with her goal in mind, she played along. Josie sunk down in her seat, and her friend beside her consoled her through the rest of the reviews. Afterward, much of the group huddled around her, too. As an outsider, Minka kept her distance but had the volume on her cochlear as high as she could tolerate it. From what she surmised, Josie already informed the ladies of her recent breakup, but none seemed to be privy to the details.

Minka planned to leave when Josie did, which forced her to stay longer than she would've liked. She munched on snacks to avoid suspicion, until her target headed out to the parking lot. She followed her, reminded of Wes's comparing her to a stalker. Josie's car occupied a spot close to the entrance, so she managed to casually approach her along the way.

She initiated the conversation before the woman could duck into her vehicle. "I enjoyed your speech."

"It didn't consist of much." Josie seemed more embarrassed than she had earlier.

"It was more than I gave. I'm Minka, by the way."

"Josie. I would've liked to hear your thoughts."

"Thanks, but public speaking intimidates me. The unrequited love storyline drew me in, too. I suspect we've all experienced it at some point, in varying degrees."

Josie pursed her lips, nodding, and for a moment, Minka didn't expect her to say any more. Nonetheless, she stood still, and her patience paid off.

"Most times, I've played the bad guy in those scenarios. I guess I send the wrong signals, which probably helps me excel in PR. I like to employ manipulation techniques. In my latest relationship, though, I found myself on the opposite end and discovered how much it hurts."

"Was he a lot like Theodore?"

"Pretty much. He didn't have any other women, at least to my knowledge. His work was his mistress, and I finally had enough. It took me being left alone at a bowling alley to get there, but I did."

Minka sucked in her desperation, restraining her arms from grabbing her to shake a better explanation out of her. "He took you bowling and deserted you?"

"Yes. A friend of his visited from out of town, and my boyfriend claimed he wanted us to meet, but he didn't do more than introduce us before they split off by themselves. They never even played, unless they did after I left. He directed me to wait at the bar, but after two drinks, I stormed outside and called a cab."

Minka wanted to ask if she'd spoken to him since, but Josie became distracted.

"I forgot my purse inside. I'd better run in for it before they lock up. Nice to meet you, Minka."

She reciprocated and started to stroll to her SUV. Upon noticing that Josie had left her door open with her phone on the driver's seat, she peered around and grabbed it when she verified no one was nearby. With the phone unlocked, she tapped on her text messages app in haste. She scrolled down to her chain with Hamilton and their dialogue on the night in question. She discovered his invitation to go out with him, followed by a brief exchange after Josie lost patience.

He realized her absence at three minutes past nine.

—*Where are you?*—

—*I busted out of there half an hour ago. Your buddy and so-called business seemed to amuse you better than I can.*—

Hamilton didn't reply and would be assaulted

minutes later. Josie apparently didn't get word of it for two days, during which she sent him repeated appeals to talk. She may have engaged in a romantic relationship with her boss, but she didn't batter him.

****

As she drove home, Minka contemplated Josie's date with Hamilton and envisioned the scene. She could imagine her sitting alone, lonely and bored, but wondered what preoccupied the CEO for so long. People often invited friends along to bond with a new love interest and merge their social circles, but why tend to business concerns on such an occasion? Plus, what kind of business could he accomplish at a bowling alley with a friend who lived so far away?

After she returned home and spent some time with Wes, she decided to research Hamilton's buddy. She remembered his name was Steadman Rissdale and typed it into the search box, which led her to his company, Riss Software. In every sense of the word, it mirrored Stags Technology, with its products and services similar to the ones featured on Stags' website. Upon her further examination, she learned that Riss had boasted more sales than Stags had the prior year, in spite of it being established almost a decade later.

Operating in different countries, they probably didn't pose much of a threat to each other, but it surprised her to note Hamilton's name on the list of Riss Software's shareholders. More brow-raising than that, a recent press release announced the construction of a new branch in Orlando. Why would Hamilton invest in the competition, much less usher it to his own backyard?

The corporate world always puzzled her, so she

didn't strain to understand it at the late hour. Regardless, it explained what occupied the two and stole Hamilton's attention from Josie. But why conduct such business at a bowling alley?

Her day of speculation wore her out, making her sleep better than she had since Robin's arrival. Her Thursday morning showed promise, with her decreased anxiety level seeming to rub off on Caela, who didn't even cry when she woke. For a whole twenty minutes, cheer bloomed in the Avery household...until her brother entered the room.

With his hair a mess and pajamas full of holes, Robin stumbled into the kitchen and uttered a groan. His demeanor didn't surprise Minka, as he greeted most days the same way when they attended school. She remained calm and tried to treat him like she'd observed her mother do—albeit without the terms of endearment.

"What would you like for breakfast?"

"An omelet," he grunted.

"I think we're out of eggs. I'll buy some today. Is cereal all right?"

"Whatever."

Though his lack of gratitude and manners grated on her nerves, she kept her cool. "Did you sleep well?"

"Nah, I never do in that basement."

Her anger began to take shape. "The garage couldn't have offered much more comfort."

"The back seat of your car isn't so bad."

She gritted her teeth and mumbled, "Then, why'd I bother carting a mattress down all those narrow stairs?"

"You tell me." His exceptional hearing had always compensated for her lack thereof.

"You are just a ray of sunshine today."

"Don't blame me. My meds ran out three weeks ago."

His statement floored her. "Your meds?"

"Yeah, I take an antidepressant and anxiety medication."

"Why haven't you told me? I could've picked them up for you." She'd do anything to better his mood for everybody's sake.

"My shrink insists I visit him before he fills out a new prescription, but I'm stranded here with this stupid tracker on me."

"You're allowed to go to doctors' appointments. How long have you been seeing a psychiatrist?"

He shrugged and carried his breakfast into the living room. "Since I was a kid."

Paralyzed by the realization, Minka froze in place. A therapist had treated both of them for a year after the abduction, but she'd assumed the doctor released him at the same time she signed off on her. They moved away after her final session, and her parents had never hinted to taking either one of them to a new therapist. Sure, her mom or dad took Robin to places on his own from time to time, but she always believed their claims of going to basketball or tee-ball practice.

They were all lies, however, no doubt to protect her from the truth. As it sunk in, Minka slowly dropped to the floor, the same guilt that had plagued her at eight years old rushing back to her. She couldn't help but remember the many times she'd become angry with him over his behavior, when the whole while, he was still suffering from the trauma she'd failed to prevent.

When she rose back to her feet, her remorse made

it hard to face Robin, like she struggled to in the days after his rescue. She couldn't avoid him for long, though, having a baby waiting to be fed at the table and other errands to run. Hence, she regained her composure and resumed her day.

He scheduled an appointment with his psychiatrist that afternoon, so she drove him. In the car, she continued to reflect on their childhood and how their relationship changed after his kidnapping. She'd asked him countless times to tell her what he'd gone through, but he never opened up to her. After a few weeks, her parents instructed her to stop questioning him. Up till now, all she'd gleaned was that his abductor locked him in a basement...

The instant the thought crossed her mind, Minka rebuked herself for being such an utter fool. She couldn't believe she'd force him to stay in their basement, forgetting the nightmare he'd lived in one. For a moment, she almost convinced herself that it hadn't occurred to Robin, either, but in light of his slighting comments that very morning, she perceived it did affect him.

Ashamed, she wanted to ask him outright and beg for his forgiveness, but she resisted the impulse. When dealing with her brother, she had to handle matters with discretion.

"I was just considering how you said you can't sleep in the basement." She started to tiptoe onto the tightrope. "Does the bed bother you, or is it something else?"

Once again, he employed a deflective mechanism. "I don't know."

"We can switch some things up if it would help.

Wes and I could park outside if you'd rather be in the garage. I understand it isn't the cleanest, but you're welcome to it." She tried to conceal her grin about the cleanliness aspect.

He stared into space.

"Or I suppose we could scoot Caela's crib into our room, and you could stay in her nursery." Minka didn't like the idea, but she was desperate to drag an answer out of him.

It worked, prompting him to glare at her, but he didn't give the response she'd wanted. "Why are you being nice to me all of a sudden?"

His words stirred up a mix of frustration, humor, and confusion in her. "Well, you are on 'house arrest,' so I want you to feel at home."

"Give me a break, Minka."

With no other choice, she decided to admit a semblance of the truth to him. "I guess I just realized the challenges you've encountered in your life, and I don't want to add to them."

All at once, his face softened, and he seemed to sense that she had pure intentions. Not the sentimental type, he spun back around to gaze out the window. "I'll take the garage."

****

Minka sat in the waiting room, flipping through magazines while Caela played in the kiddie corner. Robin's appointment had exceeded his allotted hour, but subsequent to the last few weeks, she understood. Plus, the doctor didn't have any patients waiting for him, so a little overtime pay wouldn't hurt him. Regardless, she didn't mind, as long as she didn't have to pick up the bill.

In fact, the time she spent there refreshed her, almost a psychiatric treatment in itself. Of course, she still had to keep a close eye on Caela, but she didn't shoulder the same responsibilities she did at home. For once, she could sit and relax, assured her brother was in good hands. She hadn't enjoyed this much peace in weeks, despite the rocky start to the morning.

When Robin's visit approached the ninety-minute mark, Caela began to fuss, and Minka started to grow tired of reading the latest gossip and parenting tips. To occupy them both, she lifted the little one onto her lap and bounced her, while her gaze drifted to the muted television, which was tuned to a world news station. The closed captions translated the stories it was covering. She scanned it with minimal interest, but before long, a report brought her to attention:

Breaking news out of Quebec: Founder and CEO of Riss Software, Steadman Rissdale, was just escorted out of his office by police amid allegations of embezzlement. According to reports, a recent audit revealed an inaccuracy in the company's accounts, with the books boasting five million dollars that couldn't be tracked down. The sum was later found dispersed in three different offshore accounts, all linked to Rissdale. At this time, police haven't charged anyone else, but sources anticipate more to fall into the crosshairs in the coming days.

Minka gasped the instant the screen displayed the man she'd researched just a few nights ago. Questions about Hamilton's connection to the scandal raced through her mind, and she wondered if it was the scandal that consumed the men's attention during their evening of bowling. Could it be coincidence that they both would land in tumultuous situations around the same time? Minka didn't believe so.

Disrupting her thoughts, Robin emerged from the doctor's office and nodded toward the door. She picked up her daughter and followed him, but her mind continued to spin. All the way home, she pondered the possibility of the two incidents somehow being linked, but she didn't have the resources to go much further.

Had she worked on the force, Minka wouldn't have hesitated to run her theory by Cael, even if he still would've found the holes in it. Being in the position she was, however, she resolved to do her homework first. She seized her laptop the instant she had some time to herself.

She skimmed through several articles discussing Rissdale's latest exploits, many of which reiterated the same allegations the news report had. Giving up on that subject for now, she decided to dig deeper into his relationship with Hamilton. The two appeared to be longtime friends, posing in various photos together over the years at charity events and personal outings. Their life courses seemed to coincide, too, with both divorcing their wives the same year and rising in their business pursuits shortly thereafter.

Again, she reflected on Perry's involvement in Riss Software, and it didn't cease to confound her. To the best of her ability, she searched to find out if they were sister companies, but she didn't spot any indicators of it. Steadman wasn't listed anywhere on Stags' site, so Perry's investment seemed to be one-sided.

Wes bent over his wife's shoulder. "Who's Steadman Rissdale?"

Although she never liked when he snooped into her

investigations, Minka welcomed the chance to tell somebody about her theorizing. "He's Perry Hamilton's bowling buddy the night he was attacked. Ironically, he's in some sorry straights himself. He was just caught juggling the books of his software company and supposedly embezzled five million dollars. When I did some probing the other day, I discovered Hamilton was one of the company's largest investors, and it puzzled me. This takes it to another level."

"Why would he invest in a competitor?"

"That's what I can't understand. Their companies don't seem to be related or anything, but Hamilton's even been backing an effort to establish a branch here. It just doesn't add up for a good businessman to welcome a rival company to his own stomping grounds."

For a change, Wes followed her reasoning. "Unless he cares more about his own success than that of his own corporation."

"Exactly. I traced through their sales and stock, and Riss Software has been far outmatching Stags Tech in recent years. I can't help but wonder if he's submitting to his own demise. Meanwhile, he could be preparing to reemerge as one of Riss' founding fathers. People have done stranger things in the name of an ego and greed."

"True, but are you suggesting this has something to do with Robin's case?"

"I'm not sure. Even if Hamilton is involved in Rissdale's criminal activity, it doesn't mean Robin's off the hook. There's still a chance he 'just so happened' to go after his boss the same night Hamilton was visiting with his shady friend. Still, it just smells like too much of a coincidence, you know? At the very least,

Hamilton must have some insight into his buddy's schemes, and maybe that led to his assault."

"I guess it's possible, but I had a couple of friends in college who didn't have the best of records; I was hardly aware of their shenanigans."

She eyed him with skepticism. "You and I both know that isn't true."

"It is when we're talking around my daughter." He grabbed Caela off the floor and cradled her in his lap. "I appreciate your points on this mess, honey, but don't get too wrapped up in it. You have enough on your plate as it is. While it isn't ideal to have Robin here, you can't go on a desperate witch hunt trying to vindicate him and get him out of our hair."

"I'm not doing this just to kick him out the door. Sure, it'd be a perk, but that's not my motive. I may not be a cop anymore, but I still don't want someone to commit a crime and allow somebody else to take the rap for it, especially when it involves my family. How could I face my parents again if I let Robin go to prison when I doubted his guilt?"

Wes didn't argue with her reasoning, but Robin's entrance into the room ended the conversation. Minka resolved not to reveal any of the recent developments to him, hating to build up his hopes of being proven innocent. Plus, she didn't want to encourage him to sway her opinion in the wrong direction if he was guilty.

"Have you picked up my meds yet?"

"No. I had to wait until Wes was home to watch the baby."

Meds? her uninformed husband queried in ASL.

Tell you later, she signed, then said out loud, "I'll

109

start dinner, then head to the pharmacy."

"When you do," Robin said, "could you take my phone and get me some Wiki Rocks? My game's been down since I've been trapped here."

"Wiki Rocks?"

"From Wiki Revolution," the guys said in unison. Robin gave his brother-in-law a high-five.

She raised a brow at her husband. "You mean the ridiculous game that had you scouring the city for imaginary dinosaurs while I was taking care of our newborn?"

Wes grinned. "I always combined it with diaper runs."

Robin passed her his phone. "I have a couple eggs that need hatched, too, so drive slowly."

"I'll give it a go, but hatching your eggs seems a little too personal."

For the first time in years, he snickered at his sister's wit, making Minka, once again, wish they'd shared a closer bond. Her sadness evaporated, however, when he proceeded to order Wes to cart his belongings out to the garage. Unaware of that development, too, her husband leveled a puzzled expression at her, but she reaffirmed her approval of the request.

By the time she returned home, the two had already finished furnishing the space. When she hit her garage door opener, she discovered her brother lying in his bed. He raised his head and shot a perturbed scowl at her, as if she were invading his space. She was tempted to throw up a sign even he would understand, but she resisted, advising herself to stick to her word.

She plastered on a Cheshire grin, backing up and lowering the door down. "Sorry."

Despite the inconvenience she'd just encountered, it relieved her to find only Wes playing with Caela in the living room. The television wasn't blaring in the background, and the microwave didn't beep incessantly after heating up a frozen burrito. Rather, her little family passed the time in peace.

As much as she wanted to bask in the newfound solace, her thoughts continued to drift back to Hamilton's potential hand in his friend's fraud. With the scope of it, she doubted she'd be able to deduce if or how it was related to the assault and questioned if the police could, either. There was a chance the authorities in Quebec would uncover some link to Hamilton, but would it be enough to impact Robin's fate?

While her lack of a badge had been a detriment throughout the predicament, Minka realized how, in this instance, her status as a sister could work again to her advantage. In light of the allegations against her brother, she could pay a visit to Hamilton to apologize for Robin's behavior. She could take her time with him, listening to the ordeal he'd endured, all while gathering any intel she could about him. True, it wasn't a warrant, but at least it could get her through the door.

With her plot strategized, Minka headed to Stags' main branch the next morning to determine if he was back on the job. Since it was the building where Robin worked, she told the front office she wanted to collect his belongings. The secretary surprised her when she grabbed a small box from beside her and handed it over without delay, not uttering a word. The news had clearly spread that Robin was Hamilton's alleged attacker, but the disgruntled woman agreed to let Minka apologize to the CEO face-to-face.

For his part, Hamilton's demeanor was friendly, despite the bandages still covering the wounds on his face. He smiled when she entered the room, even standing from his desk to greet her with a handshake. He appeared to have made significant progress since Cael's interview with him a couple weeks prior.

Then, his voice had been weak, tremulous. Now, he welcomed her in almost a shout, apparently aware of her hearing impediment. "Hello, Mrs. Avery. It's so nice to meet you. I've admired your work with the police department."

Taken aback, Minka wondered how he knew who she was, but she reciprocated in kind. "Nice to meet you, too, sir. I'm glad you're back on your feet."

"So am I. I'm sure this wouldn't have happened if you had been on the job." She assumed he was trying to appeal to her ego. His belittling manner, in reality, did nothing for it. "Please, have a seat, and tell me why I have the privilege of having you in my office."

She bit her tongue but remained cordial. "I don't want to take up too much of your time, sir, but I'm Robin Parker's sister. I just wanted to apologize on behalf of my family for any involvement he had in your injuries."

"I appreciate that, but it's unnecessary, as far as I'm concerned. It's been a rough experience, but I've forgiven whoever's to blame." Hamilton's docile statement sounded a bit rehearsed to Minka, and so did his follow-up. "As you'd imagine, his employment has been terminated here, no matter what his future holds, but I hope you'll pass along that I wish him the best."

Minka checked out his office every time he glanced away. "That's kind of you."

"To be honest, I'm sorry for your family's suffering in all of this. I can understand how difficult it is when somebody you care about disappoints you."

She nodded, right before the CEO's phone rang. She half expected him to excuse her, since their business was pretty much finished from his standpoint, but he just rotated his chair. He greeted his caller in a much lower volume than he'd been using with her, but it wasn't close to a whisper. His misperception of Minka's limitations worked to her advantage, as it allowed her to eavesdrop without even trying. To her disappointment, it seemed to be all business that didn't involve Rissdale.

Caela let out a whimper, signaling that her patience was running out. In an attempt not to disrupt him, Minka rolled the stroller back and forth, which soothed the baby as usual. Even so, her mother figured it wouldn't last for very long and seized the opportunity to continue to visually browse the room for anything that could assist in her research. The office didn't have many personal touches, no doubt because of his lack of a wife or child. Behind his chair, she noticed a college flag, and soon after, her eyes caught the school's logo also on his bachelor's degree. Studying the framed document as best she could from her vantage point, she realized it bore a different name: Percy Hickington.

Smiling, she understood why Hamilton had opted to change his name but typed it into her phone for future reference. Perceiving that his call was wrapping up, Minka scanned her surroundings thoroughly and spotted a framed picture of Hamilton and Rissdale. She stared at it for a brief spell, until Hamilton's closing sentence beckoned her attention.

"We've taken care of it on our end, so there's no need for alarm."

The statement could've pertained to a number of subjects, but something in his manner gave her a bad feeling. She ignored it for the moment, as he apologized for the interruption.

Unable to resist another impulse, she called attention to the photo of him and his friend, playing dumb. "I recognize him from somewhere. Hasn't he been in the news lately?"

"He has indeed." Hamilton let out a sigh, which seemed more genuine than anything he'd done the whole time. "Like I said, I can understand what it's like when someone you care about disappoints you."

"I'm sorry. I didn't mean to pry."

"Once a detective, always a detective, right?"

Chapter Six

Minka exited the room moments after Hamilton's eerie though insightful words and pondered the exchange as she made her way to the elevator. His seeming despondency over Rissdale's troubles surprised her, but she couldn't say she left his office with a changed opinion of him. Over the course of just minutes, she'd observed his personality change three times, so she couldn't decipher which, if any, of them were sincere.

She punched the button to call the elevator, and an employee soon joined her as she waited. He offered a kind smile at her and Caela but said nothing. He held the door once it opened, in order for Minka to navigate the stroller into the small space, which was when she noticed the pocket watch in his hand. She caught her breath, wondering if any of the possibilities circling her mind could prove true, but she kept her hopes at bay.

She nodded to it. "That's nice. Not many people carry those anymore."

"No, they don't, but I collect them. I've acquired over three hundred, and I never get tired of them. My wife, on the other hand, disagrees."

Minka snickered as the doors reopened, tickled by more than just his wit. She endeavored to conceal her intrigue, though, in case he realized who she was. Still not sure how to interpret Hamilton's comment, she didn't want to raise anyone's suspicions of the reason for her visit. Hence, she gave him a casual goodbye but snuck a peak at the man's nametag and noted that it read Bryant Maxwell.

As Maxwell wished her a good day, he had no idea the role he would end up playing in it. On her drive home, she tried to adopt a reasonable mindset on the watch collector, admitting that he may not have bought Robin's. It was a large company, so he couldn't have been the only person capable of purchasing it. Still, it called for unusual tastes, which he clearly possessed. Considering, too, that the watch was the primary evidence against her brother, she couldn't write it off altogether.

Once home, she set the notion aside to give Caela her lunch and lay her down for a nap. Alone with her computer after that, Minka couldn't resist the urge to run a search on Maxwell. It didn't surprise her that he wasn't trending on the web, only listed on an ordinary directory and the Stags' site. From the latter, all she could surmise was he'd been a loyal employee from the company's beginning, which didn't mean much to her at the time.

She lingered on his profile page for a while, inspecting it for anything she may have missed. As she massaged her aching brow, the phone rang. At the sight of the Palettas' number, she groaned and crossed the room to grab a pain reliever.

"Minka!" Camille exclaimed the instant she answered the phone. "I was watering my garden, and I noticed a strange man trying to get into your car. Thankfully, it was locked, but then, he dashed into your garage. I almost chased after him with my hose, but I couldn't keep up his youthful speed, so I hurried in and called you. I can't take chances like that at my age."

While annoyed by the fact that Robin was messing with her car without asking, Minka expected this would happen sooner or later and gave her planned response. "Oh, that's just my brother. He's staying with us for a while. I asked him to check whether or not I remembered to lock my doors."

"What a relief. I'd hate for anything to happen to you guys, especially to that precious little girl of yours. Your brother is living with you, then? Where's he from?"

"Here, there, and everywhere." Minka couldn't admit he lived only twenty minutes away, certain it would ignite Scoop's suspicions. "He's in between jobs right now, so we're trying to help."

"Oh, bless you. It's a shame when kids grow up to be that unstable." Her remark gnawed at Minka's nerves, given Camille had taken a disliking to her parents for no reason over the years. "I'm sure he's so grateful to have a dependable sister like you."

"That's how my folks raised me," she reciprocated with a smooth counterblow, grinning. "Well, I appreciate your concern, Mrs. Paletta. Give your husband our best."

"Same to yours. I'd like to meet your brother sometime. Maybe I can help him find his way."

His way to the loony bin, maybe. As she ended the call, she brushed off her irritation with her neighbor and headed for the garage, armed with her new ammunition against Robin.

"Why were you nosing around my car?"

"I just remembered I'd left my soda in the door

yesterday and wanted to finish it. Then, I caught a glimpse of my box of stuff in your back seat. What were you doing with that?"

With the tables turned on her, Minka had to do some quick brainstorming. "I just picked it up at Stags for you."

"Did they call you or something?"

She refused to reveal her true plan yet. "No, I was in the area, and the idea occurred to me."

Despite his accusatory manner, he accepted the explanation without hesitation and asked for another snack. Relieved to be off the hook, she invited him in and offered him a sandwich. She'd failed to close her laptop on the kitchen table, distracted by Camille's call and whatnot, so she nearly leapt out of her skin when he plopped right down in front of it.

"Why are you on the Stags site?"

"Just browsing." It wasn't a part of her original plan, but she decided to improvise. "By the way, do you recognize him?"

Robin regarded Bryant's picture for a second, before he said no more than the caption underneath it. "He's one of the accountants."

"Did you ever meet him?"

"Yeah, a few times. Why?"

Fighting the temptation to return his elusiveness, Minka had to remind herself of her goal. "As a matter of fact, I bumped into him when I picked up your things."

Robin's inner child kicked in before his sister could proceed with her impromptu interrogation. "About that, did you get my Farmer Jeffey bobblehead?"

"I don't know. They just handed me a box, and I put it in my car. Tell me more about this Maxwell guy."

"There's not much to tell. Can I have your keys so I can get that box and my drink?"

With his attention span shorter than her infant daughter's, Minka figured she'd better cut to the chase. "Is he the one who bought Papa's watch?"

His eyes widened. "How'd you figure that out?"

"He was using one a lot like it and mentioned that he collected them."

After a moment, Robin nodded. "He'd been begging me for it ever since I let him appraise it. His offer rose about every month, but I didn't want to give it up unless I had no choice. Finally, it happened. He must not have wanted it too badly, though, since he lost it right away."

"Must not have." Despite agreeing, Minka didn't believe it was really that simple.

****

Minka fessed up to Cael about her detective work over the phone.

"So, you waltzed in there and played 'Scoop.' "

She bristled at the comparison. "That isn't the point. I found out who bought the watch off of Robin. All you have to do is talk to him and determine how it ended up at the crime scene."

"Get real, Minks. I mean, if he planted it there, he isn't going to tell us that. Plus, there's no evidence he ever had it in his possession. It's still just Robin's word against his."

"It can't be 'against his' until you go over and talk to him."

She had him cornered. "I'll run through some

options with Declan, but I can't promise anything."

With that, he hung up the phone and sighed, faced with quite a challenge. It wasn't easy calculating his next move, as going after this so-called lead seemed rather pointless. If it were given by anybody else, he wouldn't even be considering it, deeming it just another frantic attempt to exonerate a loved one. Given Minka's background on the force—along with the fact that she was his sister-in-law—he was willing to yield to her instincts.

Cael supposed he could act like the watch was recovered and traced back to Maxwell, but explaining the details would be tricky. He hadn't reported it missing or stolen, and even if he had, they couldn't hand it over with it being a piece of evidence. While testing it for DNA could prove helpful, Maxwell could claim to have been merely admiring it if any of his fingerprints were detected.

Cael decided checking for prints would be the best place to start and admitted it should've been done when it was first recovered. With Robin's initials on it and Cael's connection to Minka, it hadn't seemed necessary at the time, but in retrospect, they should've taken the precaution. Thankfully, he had a friend in the lab he sometimes called upon when in a pinch like this. Most of the time, her findings corroborated what he'd already discovered, but that wasn't so in this case.

"There was only one set of prints on it."

That didn't surprise him, and he waited for her to say Robin's name.

"His name is Jevon Hinckley," the technician said.

The unexpected response took him aback as he recalled Hinckley was the one who'd showed up with the watch. It took a moment for him to absorb the meaning, but once he did, he calculated its implications on the investigation. With neither Robin's nor Maxwell's fingerprints on the piece of evidence, someone must have wiped it clean before dropping it in that alley. This had to be more than the work of an ordinary, clumsy criminal.

Cael pondered the possibility of Robin wiping off his own prints, but it didn't add up. No savvy perpetrator would leave behind such incriminating evidence at a crime scene, with his initials engraved on it and all. His own sister was a former detective, so Robin would have to expect she'd be called in to identify it. Everything considered, none of it made sense...unless whoever put it there wanted Robin to take the blame.

If that were the case, the questions arose of who would be framing him and why. The likeliest candidate was Maxwell, based on Robin's claim to have sold the watch to him. That would give him the means to plant it at the crime scene, but Cael couldn't rationalize his possible motive. Maxwell held a position in a different department and had much more seniority than Robin, so he shouldn't have envied his co-worker for professional reasons. Besides, Robin's track record was propelling him anywhere but a promotion.

With that track record in mind, he figured, that in itself could've led Maxwell to frame him. He could imagine that Robin's lackluster work ethic and overall demeanor had netted him some enemies. The accountant, in particular, could've viewed him as a waste of money and decided implicating him in a criminal investigation would be a way to get rid of him for good. That isn't to say he was the one who attacked Hamilton, but he could've seized the opportunity to blacken Robin's already tarnished name.

Cael put the brakes on his speculations, reminding himself he had too many "ifs" and "could haves" and not enough facts. He supposed the best place to resume his search was with the resource he had, Jevon Hinckley. He and Declan had vetted the stranger after he'd surfaced with the watch, but they hadn't gone much further than checking if he had any connections to Stags or Robin. This case was continuing to prove, however, that not everything was as tidy as it appeared.

Hinckley had a record, consisting of a DUI and a robbery charge. Both took place three years earlier, leading one to assume he'd changed his ways since then. Given that he didn't live in the best part of town and was unemployed, it wasn't a stretch to conclude he was hoping for a payday when he found the watch, which was why Cael and Declan had shrugged off his motives. In hindsight, Cael realized if he were after financial gain, he probably would've pawned it instead of taking a chance on a reward. Besides, guys with his profile didn't typically set foot in a precinct without handcuffs on their wrists or something up their sleeve.

With all of this spinning in his head, Cael began to picture another scenario, in which Hinckley was hired to hand over the watch. It made perfect sense, considering his lack of work, but it was yet another theory with no proof. He searched again for any connections to Stags or Maxwell but didn't stumble on anything. From there, he explored Hinckley's social media profile. His three most recent posts showed him with a sports car he'd just purchased. The model appeared to be a few years old, but he still couldn't imagine how the unemployed man could've afforded it.

He chose to clue in his partner across their shared desk. "Hey, Dec, do you remember what that Hinckley kid drove here when he turned in Robin's watch?"

"An old, beat-up station wagon."

He clicked on the first photo of Hinckley posing beside his new ride. "Nothing like this, huh?"

Declan took the phone from him and enlarged image, immediately drawing out the car fanatic in him. "No way. This baby is loaded. I begged my parents for this very model when I started driving. It may be over twenty years old, but it holds its value because it was an anniversary edition. I loved the T-top, and that cherry red is original. The scoop hood would've been added by either him or a previous owner. When did he get it?"

"The picture is time-dated the day after he came here. He must've run into some dough."

Declan nodded. "Depending on how many miles it has on it, I'd say he paid at least eight grand. Wasn't he unemployed?"

"Sure was. Look at the comments. Someone asks, 'How'd you get your hands on that beauty?' and he replies, 'Right place, right time.' It doesn't sound like he saved up hard-earned cash to me."

"Me neither," his partner agreed. "Are you saying this is connected to the watch?"

"All I know is I just sent the watch to the lab to run prints, and Hinckley's was the only set they found, not Parker's."

Declan handed Cael's phone back to him. "But Minka confirmed it as his. It even has his initials."

"It is his, but somebody wiped off his prints. It

could've been Parker, but that would mean he ditched it at the scene on purpose. Why would he do that?"

After giving it some consideration, Declan nodded. "You're right; something's off. How do you suggest we handle it?"

"For starters, we should go congratulate him on his buy," Cael said.

****

Cael and Declan set off to track down Hinckley, beginning at his apartment. Not to their surprise, many of the locals scattered when Cael approached the curb. The car that'd sparked their curiosity was parked in front of them, and Hinckley just so happened to be polishing it.

Cael whistled in admiration of the vehicle. "Sweet ride."

His posture straightened, letting on to his defensive attitude. "I swear, it's mine. I can show you guys the title."

"No need, man. We just wanted to ask you a few more questions about that watch you turned into us."

He squatted to work on the tire rims, his focus on the wheel, not the detectives. "Fire away."

"In case you didn't know, it's connected to an assault," Cael said. "The only prints on it are yours, so you're now a person of interest in our investigation."

Hinckley stood and sprayed some more polish on his rag, still refusing to face them. "I don't know anything about that. I just picked it up and turned it into you. Why would I do that if I had any part in whatever happened?"

"We wondered the same thing," Declan admitted. "This nice ride might've given you the nerve."

Hinckley gave no reply, so Cael used persuasion to motivate him to cooperate. "With your prints being on it, we could charge you with evidence tampering right now. If you didn't play a part in the crime committed, I suggest you tell us the truth."

Hinckley stared down at the rag in his hand. "I might've had some help in finding that watch."

"Meaning what?" Cael asked.

"Someone else paid me ten grand to give it to you, but I didn't ask any questions. I was hurting for cash, so I just agreed."

"Did you know this guy?" Declan inquired.

"No, I just met him on my way out of the unemployment office, and he offered me the deal. I didn't even get his name."

"Can you give us a description?"

"Light hair, glasses, about six one, late thirties."

Recognizing the description, Cael took out his phone and located his research on Bryant Maxwell. "This isn't the guy, is it?"

"As a matter of fact, it is."

****

"So, Robin was framed," Minka concluded as they waited to be seated for dinner.

"Don't get ahead of yourself, Minks. We still don't have enough to exonerate him."

"You don't have enough to convict him, either. I mean, the watch was all you guys had to tie him to the crime scene. If he wasn't already arrested, he'd be free to go now."

"But he has been arrested, and that complicates everything. Besides, we can't prove he sold it or that he didn't wipe off his own prints."

"But Cael—"

"Minks, I'm tired of talking about this. As it is, I'm sidelining another case to follow up on it. We're going visit Stags on Monday to shake what we can out of Maxwell. Rest assured, this isn't over. For tonight, though, I want to put it all aside."

With his tone firmer than usual, it took Minka aback. She understood, aware of the need for down time in such a demanding job. That said, a part of her was hurt by his brisk manner, having witnessed that side of him only a handful of times. They didn't sing each other's praises all day long, but they almost always spoke to one another in a respectful way.

She let him off the hook, however, when she considered the setting and mixed company around them. Autumn held onto his arm, standing next to her folks and younger sister, who'd all driven up from Key West for the weekend. It was the first time the Avery and Hastings families had mingled among one another, causing both of the lovebirds to act somewhat on edge. Minka decided to give her brother-in-law some slack, remembering how nervous she was the first time Wes met her parents.

It wasn't long before the hostess escorted their party to the table Cael had reserved in the rear room of Orlando's top restaurant. The Friday crowd packed the eatery, especially around their table, which overlooked Little Sand Lake. Most of their neighbors were of an older demographic, making for a more pleasant atmosphere than in the Spring Breakers' Section— otherwise known as the bar.

Everybody was getting along well while they enjoyed their meals, with the exception of Autumn's sister, Shiri, and Declan, who made it obvious he'd tagged along to flirt with her. Minka couldn't pay much attention to his shameful pursuit of her, having her hands full with feeding Caela her baby food while scarfing down her own filet mignon. They'd both barely finished before their waitress rolled over the dessert cart.

Each of them picked out their own treat, except for Autumn, who was given her key lime pie by Cael. The chatter continued as normal, but Minka noticed her in-laws and Autumn's parents all casting their attention on Autumn with eagerness. Even Wes gave frequent glances her way. Minka began to suspect the reason, which became clear when she let out a shriek after cutting off a bite that held more than sweets. It captured the whole room's intrigue.

She picked the sparkler up off the dessert plate. "Oh my goodness!"

Cael rose from his seat to take a knee. "I know we haven't been together that long, sweetie, but I'm already convinced I want us to be. So, in front of our two families, will you be my wife?"

"Yes!" Autumn shouted with glee.

Stunned, Minka applauded with the rest of the crowd and tried to put on a happy face. Deep down, however, she was hurting because of her lack of knowledge. Wes's expression affirmed her hunch that Cael had shared the secret with him, and she could tell Declan had received the memo, too. She understood why Cael would've clued them in, but she couldn't wrap her head around why he didn't inform her. Besides Wes, Cael was her best friend, and she couldn't believe he would keep this from her.

Nonetheless, she continued eating her peanut butter chocolate mousse, all while Autumn flashed her ring around the table. Minka gawked like she was expected to and congratulated the bride-to-be, but she couldn't lock eyes with Cael. From the single glimpse she took of him, she could surmise he realized how his silence affected her. Uncertainty lined his face, appearing to wonder what she might say. She kept her pain concealed, not wanting to dampen the occasion.

Once finished with dessert, she handed Caela over to Wes and stepped outside the restaurant to get some air. As she strolled around the nearby shopping center, she searched for answers that only time could give her. She pondered the years she'd spent around Cael and the special bond they'd developed, one she hadn't shared with anyone else, not even with her own brother. Cael always seemed to perceive what she was thinking—for better or worse—and rather than judging her for it, he just tried to be the partner she needed.

She still chuckled inside when she reflected on the day they first met.

Reporting to the Orlando precinct for the first time was hands down the most terrifying moment of Minka's life thus far. She'd been hired in Atlanta straight out of the academy, but her excitement overpowered her nerves on her first day there, being caught up in fulfilling her childhood dream. Sadly, however, it'd proven to be her worst nightmare, which was the primary contributor to her fears now.

From day one, Atlanta designated her as a glorified page and deemed her unfit for regular police work. It frustrated and disappointed her for the year she spent there, but in the end, it set her up to answer Lieutenant

Channing's telephone call when he enlisted their assistance in tracking down his missing cousin. Despite her speech impediment, he trusted her judgement enough to unofficially assign her the case after her colleagues had refused it. She'd lived up to his expectations, locating the young woman and rescuing her from danger, which earned her a personal invitation to work for him.

Hence, she had every reason to waltz in with confidence, but she couldn't. Instead, her doubts about staying on the force and transferring precincts continued to taunt her, given she was living in a hotel with nothing in her savings after the cost of her flight. She worried her new commanding officer's kindness would soon wear off, and she'd once again be treated as nothing more than a symbol of the department's "equal opportunity" philosophy.

Nonetheless, she smiled when she ventured inside and was greeted by Gus. Following him to his office, she noticed several glances, but none captured her attention like that of the lean officer with light brown hair across the room. He observed her with intent interest, but contrary to many of the other stares she'd received through the years, his was neither impolite nor unsettling. Rather, he manifested, not only intrigue over her arrival, but a gentleness unlike she'd sensed in anybody before.

She kept her attention fixed on the young lieutenant, listening to his tutorial about how business operated. He took her into his office and handed over her uniform, complete with a small metal badge reading Officer Parker, which was more than Atlanta had offered.

That wasn't the only surprise Gus had in store for her. "I reckon that covers everything," he concluded his narrative. "I'll introduce you to your partner and then let you two get to work."

"My partner?" It stunned Minka that anyone would agree to such a task. Her former coworkers had considered her a flight risk.

"Yes, his name's Cael Avery. I figured you'd be a perfect match, since his brother teaches at a school for the deaf and can help him learn some sign language."

And there's the catch, or so Minka thought. She could imagine how the poor guy felt, being assigned to be her partner based on his brother's occupation. If they were anything like her and Robin, they probably couldn't get through a meal without arguing, let alone play teacher and student. His disdain for his brother would translate onto her, dooming their relationship from the very start.

Her rash notions were put to rest when she and Gus entered the break room and the kind-faced officer who'd been peering at her earlier awaited her. He reciprocated her timid smile, and despite not wanting to get ahead of herself, her anxiety began to fade away.

"You must be Minka." Cael extended his hand to her. "I'm excited to work with you. I hear we lived in the same town back in the day."

"Really?" She couldn't believe Gus would've told him about her family's short stay in Altamonte Springs.

He nodded. "Do you remember which street you lived on?"

"No, I was just a toddler. I doubt that even my parents do. They've moved about a dozen times since then." Still fighting her nerves, she reproved herself for divulging the useless tidbit.

Gus excused himself and left the new partners staring at each other, lost for words. Finally, Cael offered to make her a cup of coffee and put his lunch bag on the counter as he prepared it for her.

"What's for lunch?" she asked in an attempt to break the ice.

"Mac 'n' cheese and chocolate milk."

Though they'd just met three minutes ago, Minka couldn't repress her automatic retort. "What are you—five?"

Cael raised one eyebrow, seeming a bit alarmed by her bluntness, but he didn't hesitate for long. "I'll need my brother to teach me the sign for 'Mind your own business.' "

Minka muttered the phrase under her breath, recalling several of the occasions when he indeed used it on her. As much as she always cherished their friendship, she didn't appreciate how dearly she held it to her heart until after they stopped working together. Due to her disability and how often her family moved, she hadn't formed many relationships throughout her life. Thus, she'd grown protective of their relationship, and even if she hated to admit it, she viewed Autumn as a threat to it.

Wes met up with her on her trek back to the building with Caela in his arms. "You okay?"

"I guess so." Minka kept her head down, unsure of how much she wanted to confess. "There's just a lot to take in tonight. I did not expect that proposal."

"Me, neither."

"Yes, you did. I could sense it from the way you kept peeking at Autumn."

Caught, his lips formed a guilty smile, the one his wife hated to love. "He just needed a few tips. Like him, I proposed to a girl who was way out of my league, and he wanted advice on how I enticed her to say yes."

"She's wondered the same thing at times." Minka smirked, too stubborn to relent to his charm. "I guess I'm just fighting insecurities about my relationship with Cael. He has a new partner and now a fiancée, and where does that leave me? Am I merely going to be his brother's wife and niece's mother?"

"Never." He stroked his finger on her cheek. "You're Minka. I think that speaks for itself."

She smiled, touched by his sentiment, but it didn't conclude her quandary. "I'm ashamed to let jealousy control me like this. I'm thirty, with a husband and child of my own."

"You two are close. It's understandable."

"I suppose. I think it's also because of my troubles with Robin. Every day now, I'm reminded of how pitiful our relationship is, and it's made me appreciate Cael that much more. I'd hate for us to go down that same road."

"I'm telling you, honey, you don't have to worry about that."

"I'm not so sure. I mean, he didn't even tell me he was going to propose. I helped Gus pick out Lola's ring, but Cael didn't even tell me he bought one."

Wes stayed quiet for a moment, appearing deep in thought. "We took a poll."

"Excuse me?"

"Cael couldn't decide whether or not to give you a heads-up, so he had us vote on it. For what it's worth, I voted for him to share it with you. It was a tight race. Caela was the one to tip the scales."

"Oh, was she now?" Minka giggled, taking back her baby.

Chapter Seven

As Minka and Wes roamed back into the restaurant, they crossed paths with Cael on his way from the restroom. He seemed a little tense when he noticed her, so she offered him a hug and congratulated him again, being more sincere this time. He relaxed in his stature and appeared relieved that he had her approval. She still wished he'd opened up to her beforehand and averted the uncomfortable moment, but she realized she should appreciate having someone in her life who was so sensitive to her feelings.

She extended the same concession to him by refraining from calling him for the whole weekend to allow him to celebrate his engagement. With Autumn's family in town, she figured they'd have a lot of plans and may even dive into wedding preparations. Still, she kept ruminating about the last development with the watch, and her anger brewed over the thought that her brother had been set up.

His medication had improved his mood, but she discerned the reality of his situation was beginning to sink in on him. Unlike his first few days of staying with them, he didn't joke around with Wes or watch television with him, and most of his replies to either of them consisted of five words or less. She understood that depression alone caused withdrawal, but his circumstances couldn't help. In light of Maxwell's clear fabrication, remorse struck her every time she interacted with Robin, and her conviction of his innocence strengthened.

Desperate to take Maxwell to account for his deceit, she hated having to wait on Cael and Declan to go to Stags Monday morning. Then again, she didn't hold out much hope that he'd be eager to admit to his actions. Nor did they have any more than Hinckley's words to prove that the exchange ever happened. She grasped for a strategy to nail him down about it, but she couldn't settle on one.

After dinner on Sunday evening, a gentle knock tapped on the door. Before she rushed over to answer it, Cael opened it the way he'd always done when they worked together. She half expected Autumn to follow him, but he was alone for a change.

Wes grinned at his brother, his eyes glowing with mischief. "How was the weekend with the in-laws?"

"Tiring. Autumn, Shiri, and their mom seem to think the first forty-eight hours are just as crucial to an engagement as they are to an investigation. We scouted out three venues, and they scheduled us to tour four more this week."

Wes snickered. "I'm so glad Minks doesn't have a sister."

She motioned in the general direction of the garage. "Yeah, my brother has turned out to be a real blessing."

"Speaking of him, is he within earshot?" Cael asked.

"Nope, we just ate, so he shouldn't be around until after his seven o'clock nap." She rolled her eyes. "He needs something to tide him over to play his video games all night long."

"Good. I wanted to bounce my plan for handling Maxwell off you. I didn't get to tell you much about Hinckley beyond the basics at the restaurant."

She perceived his remorse over his curtness when they talked, and though it hurt her at the time, she endeavored to relieve him of a guilty conscience. "You had a lot on your mind."

He nodded. "We had to charge Hinckley with giving a false report, but he allowed us to search through his phone to prove he doesn't have a relationship with Maxwell. Thus far, we haven't found any evidence that says otherwise, so Maxwell shouldn't be aware that we're on his trail. That gives us room to be creative, and I'd bet on that as our best strategy. I doubt he'll be very forthcoming if we just interrogate him from the get-go."

She approved of his logic. "What role do you intend to play, Detective Avery?"

"In a way, you."

She gave him a teasing poke on his chest. "We've discussed this before, Cael. You won't fit into my clothes."

"I don't need to take it that far. Since the watch doesn't have any of Robin's DNA on it anyway, I'm going to unseal it from evidence and carry it into Maxwell's office. Declan and I will pretend it belonged to our grandfather and that someone referred us to him for a fair appraisal. To make it convincing, I'd like you to give me some background on it."

Minka had to comb through her memory to recall the details her papa had told her when she wrote a report on the antique in middle school. "I believe it was made around 1865. My great-great-grandfather bought it in Boston to celebrate the end of the Civil War. He handed it down to his son, who gave it to my granddad. He, of course, passed it on to Robin, but I'm assuming you won't disclose that."

"Not until we have to. He'll figure it out when he finds the inscription, but we want to catch him off-guard and proceed from there."

She liked the ruse and had to suppress her longing to be a part of it. She appreciated his diligence, but she couldn't ignore the matter that bothered her most. "I don't mean to irritate you or overstep, but I still don't understand what grounds you have to sustain the charges against Robin. You've determined now that the watch wasn't found at the crime scene, and even Hamilton said he wasn't sure if they talked beyond a brief exchange, right?"

Cael lowered his gaze, and her spirits followed suit. "I'd hoped not to mention it until we closed in on more answers, but we had his baseball bat tested. Like the watch, it didn't have any fingerprints on it, but bleach was detected. We also ran it by the medical examiner, and she said Hamilton's injuries were consistent with those inflicted by a bat of that size. I realize it's a pretty broad pool, but with everything else considered, we can't let him off the hook without something more conclusive."

The development disheartened her, but she was compelled to address another aspect of it. "Please, tell me you didn't suspect I cleaned it when I snooped around his place."

"Never. If you'd done that, you would've taken that photo from the trash. I'm sure you didn't miss it."

"How could I? It was all he had in there."

Wes gave them a bewildered frown. "What are you two talking about?"

"You didn't clue him in on your treasure hunt?"

She shrugged. "He never let me in on his."

****

Monday morning, Cael and Declan strode into Stags and asked if they could speak with Maxwell. The conversation they faced would be tricky since they couldn't present evidence of the watch ever having been in his possession. Even if they could, they had nothing to connect him to Hamilton's assault. At best, all they could gather was that he may have had it out for Robin.

Upon entering the room, they found the accountant had just arrived, still unpacking his briefcase. "Mr. Maxwell?" Cael tapped on the open door.

He raised his head and stepped around his desk. "Yes?"

"We don't mean to take you away from your work, but we just had a question for you."

"No problem. How can I help?"

"This isn't related to your job, but you have quite the reputation for watches. We've visited several jewelers, and they all threw out your name. You see, our grandfather willed us his pocket watch, and while we'd love to keep it, we could use some extra cash for his final expenses. Like I said, we've been to a few jewelers for an appraisal, but they're not offering a lot because his initials are engraved on it. Rumor has it you're not bothered by things like that."

"Not at all. In my opinion, those features add character."

"In that case—" Cael dug out the watch and passed it to him. "Does it catch your eye?"

Maxwell admired the front plate and examined the clock's face inside, therefore missing the monogram on the back. "You have no idea. This is a classic. I'm guessing mid-nineteenth century?"

"1865, as we remember. Our grandfather bought it to celebrate the Union's victory."

He continued to marvel at it. "What a timepiece."

Cael and Declan exchanged a look of surprise that the collector didn't recognize it. When Maxwell flipped it over and spotted the inscription, though, he didn't mask his alarm. He almost dropped it upon his epiphany.

"Something wrong?" Declan asked.

"Oh, I just realized this particular model was from a bad batch." He clumsily handed it back.

"Are you certain of that?" Cael asked. "Grandpa always boasted that he never had to get it serviced for anything."

"They have a defective regulator, and since it was such a mass issue, you can't find a good replacement. It's a miracle it's still ticking," he claimed.

"Really? I've done plenty of research, and I haven't run across any complaints like that," Declan disputed.

"Me, neither. Are you sure there's nothing else you dislike about it?" At that, Cael whipped out his badge from his pocket.

With sweat glistening from his brow, Maxwell took a moment to respond. "I don't know what you're getting at, fellas, but I don't trust cops who don't disclose their true identities. I'll have to excuse you so I can call my lawyer…and maybe your commanding officer."

****

"So, we've entered the 'attorney zone,' where everyone shuts up," Minka stated, folding laundry while Cael ate his lunch at her kitchen table.

"Pretty much." He again picked up the teething ring Caela kept dropping on purpose to amuse herself. "It could be worse. He could've just played stupid and sent us on our way."

"Which is what his lawyer will tell him he should've done, especially when he learns how little you have on him. Do you think he'll call Gus?"

"I doubt it, considering how we complied right away, but I wouldn't chance it again unless we have solid evidence against him." He let out a sigh. "Regardless, I gave the boss a heads-up on my way here. He has our backs."

With both of them frustrated, they remained quiet for a few moments, until Minka changed the subject. "Does Autumn have a venue tour booked for you tonight?"

"No, but she scheduled us to meet with a wedding planner. I'm not thrilled to have another woman in the mix, tossing out ideas without having to pay for them."

Minka chuckled. "I had my fill planning one wedding."

"Thank you. We're hoping for October. Do you suppose Caela will be old enough to be a flower girl by then?"

As her rascally daughter thrust down her teething ring yet again, she smiled. "I'd say she can handle scattering the petals."

Their attention was still on the little one when Robin entered the room to inform his sister of what he wanted her to add to her grocery list. Cael greeted him after he'd finished, only to receive a mumble in return. Minka rolled her eyes at her brother-in-law.

"Hey, Robin," Cael called as he began to dart off with his potato chips. "Would you mind refreshing my memory about that guy who bought your granddad's watch?"

Robin's eyes signaled his distrust. "He was just one of my coworkers. I might remember his name now. It was something like Bryan Maple."

Doubting he'd already forgotten Maxwell's actual name, Minka suppressed a laugh at his poor acting job.

"I'll check into that," Cael said. "Were you two at work when you sold it to him?"

"Yeah, I approached him in his office and asked him what he'd pay me for it."

"Was he alone?"

Robin nodded. "He was on the phone, though."

"With whom?" Cael and Minka begged in unison.

"I don't know. I had a lot on my mind," he told them in an irritated tone. "Why does this even matter now? I'm just trapped here, waiting to be convicted so I can be trapped somewhere else."

"Nice way to put it, Mr. Gratitude," Minka snapped.

"Minka," Cael rebuked her.

"It's okay, dude. I'm used to it." Robin retreated to the garage.

After her brother slammed the door, she ordered Cael, "Don't even bother trying to exonerate him. He doesn't deserve it. Jail could teach him a thing or two."

Cael gave her shoulder a squeeze on his way out. "I haven't been doing it for him."

****

At her wits' end, Minka obeyed when Wes returned home and advised her to stay in their bedroom while he took over with cooking dinner and caring for Caela. Her mind, however, couldn't rest. Instead, it kept mulling over every syllable Robin had spoken since his arrival, each annoying her more than the last.

Wes joined her after he put Caela to bed, and his presence soothed Minka's anxieties. After she had finished venting about her day, they reverted back into their normal patter, the foundation of their love. He shared stories from work he hadn't had a chance to tell lately, all of which made her laugh. He lived up to his reputation of always perceiving what she needed, both emotionally and physically, and for the first time in weeks, she fell asleep smiling.

The romance and levity wore off all too soon, though. Tuesday morning, Cael texted her to say that they lacked the needed evidence to obtain a warrant for Maxwell's phone records. Since they couldn't narrow down who he was talking to when Robin offered to sell him the watch, they still had no proof he ever bought it.

Robin's trial wasn't set to begin for another three months, so Minka wasn't optimistic with regards her foreseeable future. The developments with the watch had given her hopes of an early release, but that no longer held any promise. They'd circled back to square one, with his freedom—and her own—gone, unless another guilty party was discovered.

Throughout her day, she replayed the case in her mind over again, much like she had when she was on

142

the force. In light of all that had happened, she could hardly accept that it hadn't been a month since Hamilton's assault. In her pondering, she stumbled upon a stone left unturned, a stone that had the potential to break through the brick wall in front of them.

Caught up in trying to find a connection between Maxwell and the watch, she'd almost forgotten her other findings from her visit to Stags, such as Hamilton's real name and his alma mater. To save time, she typed both into the search box, hopeful it'd weed out the other Percy Hickingtons, if there were any. Just one page of results appeared, giving her hope that she'd locate the information she needed. She skimmed past the typical ads for information on the man, none of which showed any potential to help her, until she spotted an article on his former university's website.

Written a month before the start of the new millennium, it chronicled the school's most notorious disgraces in a series of reflective editorials. It was a short list, since the college had pretty much steered clear of controversy, with the exception of a few brow-raising incidents. The majority related to sports, detailing cheating allegations against players and one involved a coach. Even those failed to top the list. The one that merited the most backlash was a feud between roommates, one of whom was Percy Hickington.

According to the report, the occurrence took place in the mid-1980s, when the millionaire-to-be was an undergrad. He and Toby Mead were best buds throughout the semester—up until they began sharing a house. Others in their inner circle claimed there was friction from the start, but none believed it was too serious until Hickington showed up to class one day with a black eye, bruises, and a lawsuit against Mead.

Though Mead had been suspended from the campus, he maintained his innocence. He allegedly did well on the witness stand during the court battle that followed. His accuser, however, did not, changing his story multiple times throughout the case, including in front of the jury. In an unforeseen twist, his lawyer dropped all the charges against Mead the same night after his client's muddled testimony.

By the time she concluded reading the articles, Minka found it bizarre that someone could "coincidentally" suffer the same injustice twice. After such a harrowing experience, one would assume he'd scram away from a confrontation. Like many back then, she doubted it even happened the first time and was growing ever more suspicious of the second. To her, it was an example of a spoiled frat boy who wanted to submarine a source of irritation, and she could envision her brother being just that to him now. She wondered if Hamilton—aka Hickington—was trying the ploy again, but with more maturity and finesse.

Disturbed to say the least, she had to determine what to do with the information. Cael couldn't do anything about it, as he bore the responsibility to figure out what happened in the instance at hand, not dredge up the past. True, it opened up the possibility of Hamilton's injuries being self-inflicted, but that was always hard to prove. It couldn't be confirmed back then, and it didn't have a great chance in the present.

More than anything, the account called his creditability into question, and that would have the most value in a courtroom. With that in mind, Minka decided to impart it to Robin's lawyer, in hopes of helping build his argument. She had her qualms about it, given he was a public defender, and based on her experience with them, she didn't expect him to offer Robin much more support than sitting next to him during the trial. Nonetheless, she dialed his number and wished he'd surprise her.

His receptionist answered the call and informed Minka that he was in court, living up to her disillusions. She released a silent sigh but related her name and phone number to the woman, who didn't promise a return call. With fading hope, she was still on her own.

She skimmed over the webpage once more and decided to research Toby Mead. She clicked on his address listing and gazed at his number for a few moments, before she grabbed her phone to place another call. The weight of her action didn't faze her, though, until he greeted her.

"Toby Mead."

She hadn't strategized a plan, so she improvised. "Hi, I'm Minka Avery, and I'm an attorney from Orlando. I have a client who's being charged for assaulting Perry Hamilton, or, as you may know him, Percy Hickington. I've learned that you two have an unusual history and wondered if you could share any details about that with me?"

He paused for a long while, his internal conflict apparent. "You have the wrong number."

****

Drained by the abrupt end to another lead, Minka put down her phone and laptop on the coffee table. Slouching back in the couch, she covered her weary eyes with her hand. Wes opened the door at that very moment and exhaled when he approached her.

"What'd he do today?"

"Surprisingly, nothing."

"You're surprised by that?" Wes retorted, playing on his brother-in-law's laziness.

"That's not what I mean." She sat up as he began to massage her shoulders. "My stress isn't about him…well, it is, but in more of an indirect way."

"Huh?"

Minka related her day's revelations and latest theory. "But without any proof Hamilton faked it that time, there's no way to accuse him of it now and convince anybody. It's just my twisted mind, formulating scenarios that might've never happened. Even if I had the right resources, people would conclude that."

"If Hamilton did lie, don't you think the guy would be eager to proclaim that?"

"Not if he was paid off."

He nodded in agreement and started stroking her hair. "I guess we'll have to leave it to chance. It doesn't mean we'll end up facing the worst-case scenario. If Robin's lawyer does his job, he'll realize they don't have much against him. Hamilton even admitted he isn't certain of his attacker."

"Robin's lawyer won't even return a call. All he does is collect the state's money."

The two sat in silence, until Wes switched on the television. Already on the news, it showed a highlight reel of the day's more minor stories. Wes held up the remote to change the channel, but Minka stopped him when the reporter said a familiar name.

"Last week, we reported the Riss Software's CEO was being charged for embezzlement. Now, the term hardly covers the crimes police are accusing Steadman Rissdale of committing. As we've exclusively learned, Rissdale's criminal activity was discovered before the books were audited, when a local bank received a string of complaints, claiming it was distributing counterfeit money.

"After a thorough investigation, the phony bills—consisting of only twenties in an effort not to be conspicuous—were tracked to Riss Software's account. That blew the whistle on the CEO's alleged scheme of depositing the cash into his business account while he funneled the real funds into his own. The audit then confirmed authorities' suspicions, which led to Rissdale's arrest."

"Didn't you say their sales surpassed Stags'? This explains it. More than half of it may have been phony."

Wes changed the station, but Minka's mind stayed on the headline. With Hamilton so involved in his rival company since its beginning, she still couldn't believe he wasn't apprised of his friend's escapades. Could he have been biding his time so he could be in line to take over the company? Perhaps that was why he wanted to build a branch in Orlando. He could have even engineered his friend's professional demise, all so he could emerge as a conquering hero.

What if Rissdale learned of Hamilton's plotting and stormed down to stop him? Could he have been the one who attacked him out of rage?

The scenarios swirled through her thoughts, but none of them offered any evidence. With nothing to tie Rissdale to the assault, nobody would investigate him. He already had a minimum twenty-year prison sentence waiting for him. Plus, only time would prove or disprove her theories about Hamilton's intentions for Riss Software.

A text from Cael moments later showed she couldn't even count on that.

—Hamilton's dead. —

****

With Cael pursuing the latest development, Minka couldn't get much out of him beyond Hamilton was involved in a car crash on his way home from work. Cael was leaving for the scene, but he didn't even disclose where that was. She consulted both her computer and television screen for further details, but nothing surfaced. Maybe Hamilton wasn't as famous as he considered himself to be.

The twist sent a blow into the case against her brother, since Hamilton wouldn't have a chance to execute his hidden agenda. They lacked evidence to clear Robin's name, including the possibility of Hamilton "miraculously" remembering who attacked him. Robin would go down as somebody who'd recently assaulted a now-deceased man, which would no doubt provoke a jury against him from the start.

Minka tempered her reeling mind, telling herself maybe it'd all sort itself out, and Robin's suit would be dropped. Regardless, she needed answers and couldn't peel her eyes away from the news reports the entire evening. A lone article was published online after the evening news concluded, but it didn't relate much past the fact that the businessman had been killed in a traffic accident after he ran a stoplight. The driver and passenger in the car he'd collided with were rushed to the hospital, both still in critical condition.

She was rereading it when Robin shuffled into the

room. "Did you wash my sheets?"

"Yeah, they're in the dryer if you want to grab them."

"No, you can." He employed the technique he'd used on their mom to get out of doing his own chores.

Uneager to carry on tradition, his sister countered, "Thanks, but I can do without unloading one load of laundry."

His scowl revealed that he understood her message but, as usual, he didn't hurry to do the physical task. Instead, he squinted at her computer. "Man, that's pretty banged up. Did a pop star get into another wreck?"

She hadn't planned to inform him about his former boss's demise right away, but Minka reckoned it didn't matter. "No, Hamilton did, and it killed him."

"Ha! Serves him right for trapping me here." His reaction didn't surprise her, but she gave him a look of reproach. He was quiet for a moment, absorbing it. "Could this make them let me go? He's dead; does it still make a difference who attacked him?"

She couldn't admit to wondering the same but shared the conclusion she'd already made. "Assault is a crime, whether the victim's here or not. It's the DA's job to act on that."

Robin said nothing in reply, his disappointment clear. A part of Minka wanted to express her sorrow, but her continued distrust of him restrained her. She recalled Cael's statement about the bleach on his bat, and even if it wouldn't help his case with the law, she wanted to give him a chance to explain it to her.

"The police have deduced that he was beaten with a baseball bat, so they checked yours. They found a residue of bleach on it. What were you trying to clean off of it?"

"Noth—"

"Skip the deflection. I need an answer."

He ground his teeth. "This crazy squirrel jumped through the window of my apartment complex and made an absolute mess of my kitchen. When I came home and discovered it, I trapped it in a corner and whacked it. It was foaming at the mouth, so I figured it had rabies or something and was scared it was going to bite me. As you can imagine, it left a mess, so I used bleach to clean off the blood and the—"

She held up her hand to stop him from elaborating. "I get the picture. Did you tell anyone else about it?"

"No way. My neighbors are all hipsters and would judge me as cruel."

Having grown up in the same family, she believed his story. Their dad had taught them both that it was wrong to let a sick animal suffer, and she believed it had to be in sore straits to retreat to his pigsty. She resisted the urge to ask her brother what constituted an absolute mess in his estimation.

She let him leave to get his laundry, and once he withdrew to the garage, she giggled at his fear of the tiny critter. Having always been husky, his size often made him appear tougher than he was. The account reminded her of his sensitive nature, and it angered her more to contemplate the scenario of Hamilton pinning this on him just to be able to fire him. Now, Robin's termination wouldn't even matter to him.

She closed her laptop, apathetic to the details of Hamilton's demise for the moment. When Cael's car stopped in the driveway an hour later, however, her curiosity surged.

"What happened?" she asked as she opened the door to him.

"He ran a stoplight."

"You drove out here at nine-thirty just to tell me that?"

He forced a grin and entered the house. "You're welcome."

"If he was on his way home, that corner wasn't unfamiliar territory. He would've expected it."

"Maybe he just sped up, hoping he could make it in time."

"I'm not buying it."

"Unfortunately, neither is his eighty-year-old mother." Cael sat down on the couch in the living room, brushing aside one of Caela's toys sticking half in, half out of a cushion. "She's insisting he suffered from permanent brain damage caused by the assault, swears that's what led to his accident, and plans to go after Robin."

"What? How can she do that? His physician cleared him to drive, didn't he?"

"We'll be investigating that. I'll warn you, though, she's out for blood."

Minka was rubbing her temples when Wes trotted downstairs. "Who's out for blood?"

"Shirley Hamilton." His brother clued him in on the rest. After he finished his play-by-play, he shifted toward Minka. "Have you told Robin what happened?"

"He caught me researching it online, so I had to. Hamilton deserved it, in his opinion."

"As a crime fighter, I'll ignore that. Just do me a favor, and don't warn him about this one. I'd pay for it if he bolted again."

Both of them agreed to keep quiet. She considered telling him Robin's story about the bat as a last-ditch effort, but she deemed it useless. Long after he headed home, she continued to despise the injustice of it all. She wasn't anxious to go to bed, where she'd just suffer through another sleepless night. Whether staring at the television or the ceiling above her, her mind would remain on her brother. For the first time in many years, she ached to protect him. She was at a loss, however, on how to do so.

After her indignation subsided, she chose to set her mind on the brighter side. She reasoned the investigation into Hamilton's death could provide them with what they needed to crack the assault case. Perhaps Cael and Declan would be granted information that would expose his true identity, if he had one to hide. For that matter, Robin's lawyer should have access to some of the victim's files, especially concerning his health. While such may not reveal his business schemes, it would be a start to gleaning insight into his life. Hence, Minka decided to follow Wes's advice and give Attorney Floyd Chemway another casual nudge in the right direction.

She had ample opportunity to do just that when the lawyer called and asked to meet with Robin, no doubt to share the bad news. In spite of the meeting taking place at her own house, she didn't have much of a chance to speak, with her brother not in any mood to listen.

"What do you mean, she's trying to get them to up the charges?" he yelped. "I was in that stinking garage when he died! I didn't run the red light—he did!"

"Calm down, son," the older man replied. "We can fight this."

"No, we can't. I'm as good as sentenced for life, because he's some millionaire mama's boy, and I'm a nobody."

Minka and Floyd said nothing, both having enough experience to appreciate his statement held more truth than they cared to admit.

Minka focused on the facts. "What charges does the mother want them to pursue?"

"First degree murder." His declaration made both their mouths drop.

"Are you kidding me?" Minka shouted in outrage. "Even if Robin did assault him, the guy lived for almost a month, and it happened on the road. That's involuntary manslaughter, at best."

"Thanks, sis," Robin snorted. "Manslaughter would read so much better on my record."

Floyd veered the discussion back on topic. "It can be classified as first degree under the felony-murder rule. Since it followed the assault charge, a felony, it can be termed first degree if the two are found to be connected."

"But I didn't do it."

"This hasn't been issued by the police, mind you," Floyd reminded them, keeping his cool. "Mrs. Hamilton is just rallying for it."

Robin crumpled his fists. "And I'll bet she has a boatload of supporters, too."

Without warning, he rose to his feet and sauntered to the door.

Inferring his intentions, Minka leaped off the couch. "Don't do it. You'll only make matters worse. If you violate your house arrest, they'll put you in jail."

"Let 'em!" he hollered and slammed the door behind him.

Chapter Eight

Minka excused herself from Mr. Chemway and raced after her brother with Caela in tow. She didn't want to take the time to unload her regular stroller from the trunk of the car, so she grabbed the buggy her aunt Sue had passed down to her. On the few occasions she'd used it, its cumbersome, old-fashioned wheels and the inability to fold it up lent to Minka's appreciation of modern-day designs. Needless to say, it wasn't cut out for a pursuit of this sort, but because it was right there in the den she made do.

She darted outside to hunt for Robin. Since he hadn't been bold enough to take her car, he couldn't have trekked far, unless a random taxi had finally stumbled across their block. He wasn't a strong runner, but she didn't want to give him much of a lead. A left turn would take him deeper into their secluded neighborhood, so Minka headed right, all while texting Cael. She figured he'd already been alerted of Robin's escape thanks to the monitor on his ankle and wanted to assure him she was handling it.

Her focus shifted between her phone and daughter, who kept wiggling and rolling onto her knees. She entreated her to stay still. In the end, the baby's persistence benefitted her distracted mother. She sat up just in time to spy their target.

"Boy!" she crowed, pointing at Robin from her

kneeling position.

From his seat on a park bench, he cast a despondent gaze on his sister. Neither said a word as Minka joined him. In the silence, the vibration of her phone was noticeable, prompting Robin to steal a glimpse of the message she'd received. The instant he spotted Cael's name, he lunged to his feet and began to take off again. She sped on to the sidewalk and cut off his path with the buggy.

"Where are you going?"

"Someplace where my sister won't rat me out."

"What are you talking about? I've had your back all along. For goodness' sake, I left a complete stranger in my house while I ran after you to stop you from becoming a fugitive."

"Yeah, right. You just wanted to trap me until your wannabe brother could capture me."

"Once again, you're wrong. I wanted to notify him that you were on the move, and I had tabs on you. That way, he might not seek you out and handle it with more force."

At a stalemate, the siblings stared each other down like characters out of a movie about the wild west. For the second time in two minutes, Minka's phone intervened, with Cael calling in. Robin swerved around the stroller.

Before he could make it far, she grabbed the handcuffs she'd slipped into her pocket at home. Though out of practice, she slapped them on with no effort, putting one on his wrist and the other on the handle of Caela's buggy.

Robin started to jostle his wrist. "Hey!"

"Settle down. You may not always act in your own

best interests, but you'd better not endanger your niece."

For a change, he obeyed her and even assisted her by commanding Caela to sit down. With the two babysitting each other, Minka managed to answer the phone on the last ring.

"Hello?" She maintained a mild tone, considering the circumstances.

"What's with your text?" Cael questioned. "What's happening over there?"

"Robin's lawyer dropped by to tell us the latest on Hamilton, and Robin stormed out of the house. I just figured his GPS alarms would be going off over there."

"I'm on the road," Cael said. "So I didn't get a notice yet. Have you found him?"

"Yeah, I'm keeping a tight grip on him now." She chose not to disclose how literal her statement was.

"I'd planned to stop by on my way back to the station, so as long as he's there with you, I'll just blame it on a technical glitch."

Minka appreciated Cael's support but getting her brother on board would be a challenge. Still trying to slip off the handcuff, he demonstrated he wasn't going back without a fight. The restraint might have done the job of keeping him in place, but she couldn't overpower him and push him the whole way back.

With no other recourse, she appealed to his heart. "After your abduction, I made you a promise in the middle of the night. I'm not sure if you heard it, but I told you I'd never let anyone hurt you again."

He lowered his somber eyes. "I heard you."

"I'll admit I haven't always followed through on that, but now I'm determined. I need you to trust me."

He nodded, and she took the chance of spinning the stroller around to return home. He complied and kept a steady pace with her without incident. As they approached the driveway, he began to tinker with the cuff again.

"This thing hurts."

"Be glad I couldn't find my Taser."

****

Minka and Robin shuffled through the front door. Once she unlocked the cuffs, he marched back into the garage, his stoic expression indicating he had no plans to reemerge anytime soon. Meanwhile, Chemway had stayed in his place in the living room and was uncomfortably tapping his foot.

"I'm sorry about that." Minka lifted Caela out of the buggy. "He's impulsive, to say the least."

"I don't blame him for being upset. I've never had a case take a turn like this. I'll be doing my share of research."

His remark sparked hope that her earlier perception of him was flawed, encouraging her to enlist his assistance. "Speaking of research, I've done some of my own, and I learned this isn't Hamilton's first time being an alleged victim of abuse."

She detailed his experience in college and inability to provide convincing testimony against his supposed attacker. Despite her reservations, she even admitted her call to Toby Mead and his unnerved response. She waited for the attorney to manifest disapproval, but he didn't whatsoever. Rather, he thanked her for her diligence and promised to review the links she gave him.

A few minutes after Chemway left, the front door

opened again. Minka expected Cael to enter. Instead, Wes stepped inside. With the chaotic afternoon, she hadn't noticed the later hour. She had yet to put the baby buggy away, so it still sat in the foyer, handcuffs dangling off the handlebar and all. He narrowed his eyes. "Honey?"

She flailed up her arms to proclaim her innocence. "Everybody's fine."

"Would you care to elaborate?"

"In total honesty, no. But in case Camille calls Child Services on me, I suppose I should."

She gave him a recap of the debacle, and several times, a repressed grin flashed across his lips. She couldn't get angry with him, finding the humor in it as she proceeded with the account. Right when she concluded it, Cael appeared in the doorway. He leveled the same puzzled frown his brother had at the stroller.

"Should I ask…"

Wes put his thumb to his chest, prideful. "My daughter made her first arrest."

Minka sprinted over and tucked the buggy back in the den at last. "Really? You're taking credit for that?"

Cael snickered. "Yeah, I don't know the details, but she'd inherit those skills from Minks and me. The honor will go to you the first time she gets arrested."

Wes laughed.

"Any news on the case?" Minka asked.

"Sort of. We subpoenaed Hamilton's medical records and confirmed his doctor evaluated him late last week and gave him the go-ahead to drive."

"So, that means Robin's off the hook?" Wes asked.

"In a way. We can't charge him, but the mother can still file a civil suit against him."

Minka shook her head. "He won't have much to give her, especially if he's in prison by the time she takes him to court."

"Thanks for the vote of confidence, sis." Robin stood in the kitchen doorway, where he'd apparently been eavesdropping. He looked to Cael. "Is there any way I can get out of this?"

"With a good lawyer, there is. Since Hamilton was cleared to drive, his recovery must have been progressing well. If the accident was medically related, like if the driving restriction was lifted prematurely, liability could fall on his doctor."

His freedom of speech surprised Minka. "You seem pretty confident, Detective."

"Today told us a lot." He shot over a look that assured her he had it under control. "We also talked to Hamilton's secretary. She said he'd spent the last few days on the road, commuting to the branch office in St. Petersburg. Yesterday was his shortest drive."

"He could've been exhausted," Wes speculated.

"Yeah, but that wasn't my fault," Robin said, sounding happier than Minka had heard him in a long time.

He gave Cael a high-five and thanked him for his work, which astonished his sister. He strolled back into the kitchen; the sounds of rustling wrappers and opening cabinets left little doubt he wanted a celebratory snack. After the raid ended and the back door closed, she smiled at her brother-in-law, aware of how much his conversation with Robin violated his training.

"How are you going to testify against him in good conscience?"

He winked. "Easy. I'll recommend Declan to take the stand."

"Where is Declan?" Wes questioned.

"At court, as a matter of fact. I think he's calling me now." He grabbed his phone out of his pocket. His expression changed when he read the ID, and he ducked out of the room before he answered.

The action put Minka on edge, making her wonder if the matter under discussion would bear any weight on Robin. She quieted her disconcerted thoughts, remembering it could relate to another case. When he returned with an aggravated grimace, her nerves kicked up again.

To her relief, Wes took the initiative to learn what happened. "Is something wrong?"

"Yes. That was the hospital. Tad and Jemma Frasier, the other victims of Hamilton's crash, were recovering there. The nurse said Tad went on a rampage this afternoon and insisted on checking both of them out. The wife's injuries were more substantial, so she should be under a physician's care. Several nurses and the floor doctor tried to reason with him, but he wouldn't listen. I guess Jemma cooperated with him and had enough strength to make it into the truck that picked them up. I have to go to the hospital and talk to the staff."

With all the other developments, it hadn't occurred to her to ask Cael about the other victims. "So you never got to interview them prior to them leaving the hospital?"

"Her condition was too unstable. I tried talking to Tad Frasier first thing this morning. He said he doesn't remember anything about the wreck."

Given the man's abrupt exit from the hospital, Minka had to question if he recalled more than he claimed. Because Cael had to leave, she didn't voice her suspicion. After he left, she returned to her cyber stalking.

She ran a search on the Frasiers. Their wedding registry from two years ago topped the results, along with their marriage announcement. She didn't have much interest in their nuptials, so she continued to browse the other results. Another article about the accident followed, and she skimmed it. It named them as victims but focused on Hamilton, highlighting his rise in the software industry and his contributions to Orlando's community and charities. To further sadden her, it also mentioned his recent assault and posed the possibility of it leading to the crash.

She almost gave up on her efforts, but just before she closed the search engine window, she spotted the next result: an obituary that featured Tad's name. She might well have disregarded it, if she hadn't noticed that it was written in remembrance of a woman named Peggy Hickington Frasier. Her eyes scrambled over the tribute, in a quest for the list of survivors. Tad was her son, one of three boys, but she rushed through his brothers' names. She had another name in mind, and a moment later, she pinpointed it on the screen.

Percy Hickington was Peggy Frasier's brother, meaning Perry Hamilton was Tad's uncle.

****

Wes shook his head once Minka finished telling him about her discovery over dinner. "So, Hamilton's own nephew crashed into his car and killed him. And I thought you had issues because of cuffing your brother to our daughter's stroller."

She balled up a napkin and threw it at him. "I worked with what I had."

In her highchair, Caela followed her lead and tossed the dirty one on her tray at Wes.

"See how you're corrupting our sweet little girl."

She winked at him, sliding a clean paper towel over to her daughter. "Jokes aside, you don't buy that it's an accident Tad and Jemma were in the other car?"

"I'm not the former detective, but in a big city like this, what are the chances?"

"They could've been headed to the same place, I suppose."

He acknowledged the possibility with a nod. She pondered whether or not Tad even realized Hamilton had been the other driver. If not, could the revelation have triggered his meltdown?

She still couldn't convince herself the wreck was a kooky coincidence. It struck her as odd from the very beginning, as the circumstances didn't fit together. This new information made it even more suspicious. Her eagerness to report it to Cael burned inside of her, but she kept it contained. She didn't want to compound his frustration over the Frasiers' getaway or thwart his pursuit to track them down.

Robin entered the kitchen for another helping of spaghetti, his mood better since his conversation with Cael that afternoon. He stayed in the garage as usual, but every time he cut through to use the bathroom or rummage around for an all-too-frequent bite to eat, he checked in with Minka and made silly faces at Caela. The whole aura of the house brightened, making Minka realize how dreary it'd been.

He sat down for a few minutes and chatted with Wes, for the most part. Observing his joviality, she wished she could relieve him of this burden for good. Although he may not face murder charges, the assault charge still remained in place. The law couldn't hold him accountable for Hamilton's death, but a jury might still hold that in their thoughts.

She excused herself from the table when Cael called. Her anticipation over what he had to share rivaled her anxiousness to relate her findings. She nearly blurted it out the instant she answered but decided to yield to him.

"What's up?"

He sighed. "I spoke with the nurses who were caring for Tad and Jemma. The entire ordeal has them baffled. The one who cared for Tad said he was good-natured and calm this morning, just concerned about his wife. Shortly after he learned Jemma was alert and stable, though, he threw a fit, yelling that he needed to get her out of there."

"Did he give them a reason?" she asked.

"He claimed they didn't have insurance, so the nurse assured him it wouldn't impact the quality of care they received and that they could get assistance. She and another aide who heard him said they perceived something else was bothering him."

Minka couldn't hold her tongue any longer. "Maybe the fact that he killed his uncle."

"Huh?"

"Tad is Hamilton's nephew."

"His nephew? How do you figure that?"

She related how she'd made the discovery and apologized for not telling him before about Hamilton's unflattering birth name.

"I wonder why he'd go to the trouble of scrubbing it from all his records, except for the certificate that hung behind him every day," Cael murmured.

"He must have assumed his inflated head would block it," Minka quipped. "I should've told you right away but forgot after I ran into Maxwell and noticed his watch. I guess 'Mommy Brain' is a real thing, after all."

"It's okay. It wouldn't have been of much benefit till now, anyways."

She veered back to the Frasiers' escape. "Did you try to hunt Tad and Jemma down?"

"Yes, Declan met up with me, and we headed to the address they gave to the DMV. It was just an abandoned old bar. We also tried to call them, but no surprise, their phones are disconnected. The hospital's going to send us their surveillance so we can determine who their getaway driver was."

The dead end made her heart sink, but she didn't want to let it on to him. "I suppose that's your best bet at finding them. Keep me posted."

He promised to before they wished each other a good evening. Throughout the night, she continued to contemplate the reason for Tad's exodus from the hospital. With Jemma in such poor condition, it didn't speak well of his love for her. As a caring husband, he should want her to have the best treatment to aid in her recovery. True, the bills added up, but like the staff told him, there were provisions for that.

She didn't hold out much hope the person who aided their escape would offer a lot of help. In many crimes, the accomplice didn't cooperate unless under pressure to save his own skin. In this instance, no crime had been committed, so they wouldn't have any bargaining chip to use. Nobody could be charged with aiding and abetting stupidity, despite the countless occasions she'd lobbied for such a law among her colleagues.

When she woke the next morning, all her invigoration over Tad and Hamilton's connection faded away. It was nothing more than another link in a chain that continued to corrode before they could reach the end. Discouraged, she didn't bother to look at her phone until after breakfast, doubting it'd provide anything of value. The moment she finally picked it up, a text from Cael dispelled her cynical notion.

—*Bryant Maxwell picked up the Frasiers from the hospital.*—

****

Minka read Wes the message as he prepared to leave for work.

"That's the guy who bought Robin's pocket watch, right? He must be pretty deep in this."

"I agree, but they won't make any headway with him until they can mount some solid evidence against him. They had a better shot at pinning him down for planting the watch than they do this. Picking up ill friends at a hospital isn't a crime."

After he finished adjusting his necktie, he kissed her. "Don't drive yourself crazy over this. I'm confident matters will get sorted out."

"I'm glad one of us is. Just don't clue Robin in about any of it. Raising his hopes prematurely could lead him to crash if things go downhill. Aunt Sue's buggy can't take another wild goose chase."

He pantomimed zipping his lips and retrieved his

briefcase on his way out. In an effort to improve her mindset, she broke out the art supplies she'd been using every so often to start teaching Caela her colors. She hadn't enjoyed art a great deal in the past and never excelled at it, but she liked drawing for her little girl, who scribbled over her sketches. She had to watch Caela closely to keep her from putting the markers in her mouth, but she cherished the bonding time.

While she attempted to shape a horse, the activity soothed her spirits. It reminded her of several of her childhood therapy sessions when her counselor made her draw. Though she hadn't understood it then, she now realized the mental benefits of the task.

Even when thoughts of the Frasiers and Maxwell drifted into her head, she maintained a more objective focus. Misgivings about Hamilton's plans for Riss Software resurged; the dots started to connect with regard to Maxwell's involvement in the matter. If Hamilton had some secret scheme going, it made sense for a longtime accountant to be privy to it.

When Cael and Declan showed up that afternoon, however, their despondent faces let on they hadn't met with much success in finding the Frasiers, let alone a corporate conspiracy.

Declan plunked down on the stairs in the foyer, his drawn expression a sign of profound weariness. "We called Maxwell's attorney, who was happy to point out that if Maxwell knew Tad and Jemma's location, he doesn't have to disclose it. They weren't responsible for the accident and aren't obligated to help with the investigation."

"It's obvious they all have something to hide," Minka concluded.

"On the bright side, the phone company finally sent us Hamilton's phone records, so we can discern if distracted driving was at play," Cael informed her.

"I'll be scouring through them on my own because he's taking the afternoon off," Declan remarked.

"Yeah," Cael murmured. "Autumn has us scheduled for tours at three wedding venues."

Presented with a chance to participate in real police work, she jumped right on it. "Would you like an extra pair of eyes on the phone records?"

The offer seemed to brighten Declan's mood. "Would you throw in lunch? I'm starving."

****

Minka had hoped Declan would open up Hamilton's phone records before they ate, but when Robin popped in to get a sandwich, she realized business would have to wait. He wore a confused expression upon spotting the detective, but Minka kept her explanation vague. With the chaotic state of the investigation, she didn't want to build his hopes.

Surprising her, Declan engaged Robin in conversation. His hesitant responses revealed his continuing suspicions of the detective. Once he mentioned the upcoming superheroes movie, however, Robin couldn't be quieted. From the little attention she paid to the exchange, she deduced Declan shared her brother's love of comics, so the chat could last for hours.

Once they finished their banter about speculated plot twists, Robin took his leave, giving her and Declan some one-on-one time. They talked over police topics for a short while before personal ones crept in without either of them trying. By the meal's conclusion, she understood why Cael and he had grown so close.

It didn't disappoint her, however, when he retrieved his tablet, ready to get to work. He proceeded to open the police database and tap on the file that held Hamilton's phone records. The CEO had several different numbers, and the first one Declan chose didn't seem to be his primary means of communication. He hardly used it for most of the year since he obtained it, but his activity gained frequency in recent weeks.

Declan scrolled to the day of the accident and found a lot of calls leading up to the collision. All the conversations were to or from the same number, which repeated time and again over the past month. He ran a search on it to identify the caller. A new excitement in his voice, he sat straight up in his chair. "This is Tad Frasier's phone number."

Minka scrutinized the entry. "According to this, Hamilton called him right before the crash. Do you think he was giving Tad instructions or something?"

"It sure smells like it, especially since he's been calling almost every hour afterward."

"Must be good cell service from the grave," she joked. "Does this mean he faked his death, or could somebody else be using it?"

"Beats me. His remains were recovered from the car. They were charred from the fire, but they matched his dental records and everything."

"The records could've been switched. A guy as rich as him could pay someone off," she speculated. "When was their most recent conversation?"

He scrolled up. "Ten minutes ago."

"Can you track his location?"

He didn't have the resources they had at the

precinct, but he managed. "Some swanky downtown hotel."

She smirked. "Want to go visit his not-so-final resting place?"

Chapter Nine

Ogling the hotel's spacious lobby, Minka gave Hamilton credit for good taste in choices of hideaways. The luxury resort welcomed their guests with towering tropical indoor plants, chic couches upholstered in suede and leather, and its own open-air market. It provided a far cozier feel than the motel Wes had stayed at when he faked his death, which he'd later described as a crime scene waiting to happen.

Men's footsteps and women's clicking heels echoed over the marble floor of the lobby. Caught up in the splendor, Minka paid no regard to the people around her—until an irritated voice spoke her name.

"Minks? Dec? What are you two doing here?" Cael quickened his pace to meet up with them but kept ahold of Autumn's hand, while a sophisticated-looking woman trailed behind them.

"We're following a lead. You're considering this for the wedding?" Minka couldn't imagine her frugal brother-in-law fronting the size of the bill this place would demand.

"It isn't on the short list."

Autumn made a face. "But it might be after we go to a couple more."

"Or after we win the lottery." He rolled his eyes. "Anyway, you have a lead? Are the Frasiers here?"

Following protocol, Declan drew Cael off to the

side. "Can we speak in private?"

Cael excused himself from his fiancée and the woman Minka assumed to be their wedding planner. Minka, of course, joined the guys.

"This had better be worth interrupting our venue search. This consultant charges eighty-five bucks an hour."

Declan stepped closer to him and lowered his voice. "Hamilton's phone activity didn't end after his crash. He keeps calling Tad, even as late as half an hour ago. I tracked it, and it originated from here."

"You can't mean—"

"Unless somebody else is using it, he didn't die in that wreck," Minka declared.

Cael shifted his weight then called over his fiancé and gave her arm a long caress. "I need to check on something. You go with Talia to the other site. I'll meet you there as soon as I can."

"But, babe, you promised nothing would take priority over this."

"Why would you tell her that? You're a cop." Minka regretted the words the instant she noted Cael's steely glare and Autumn's grimace.

"This shouldn't take long." He kissed her.

Once the two women wandered away, the trio approached the concierge desk.

"Could you help us find someone?" Cael asked the woman in front of the computer, flashing his credentials as he leaned closer. "His name's Perry Hamilton."

She typed in the name in complete ignorance. "I'm sorry, but we don't have a guest by that name. Could it be booked under someone else's in the party?"

"This might help." Cael showed her the picture of

Hamilton he had on his cell phone.

She studied it well. "Yes, I remember him. In fact, he just checked out about five minutes ago. He left suddenly. We had to charge him for an extra night, since we can't rent it out before housekeeping cleans tomorrow afternoon."

"What name did he use?" Cael questioned.

She searched in her records. "Steadman Rissdale."

The web of scenarios in Minka's mind about the buddies spun faster and took on more intricacy. "How did he pay?"

"With cash."

"I don't suppose you heard where he was headed when he left," Declan asked.

"No, I didn't."

"Did you see what he drove?" Cael posed.

"He registered a license plate number with us when he checked in."

Cael wrote down the sequence of numbers, but before they left, Minka had another idea. "Would we, by any chance, be able to access his room?"

"Why not? Let me summon my assistant to show you to the floor."

As they made their way up to the suite, Cael, via sign, reminded Minka they didn't have a warrant. Likewise, she pointed out that Hamilton forfeited his rights to the room when he checked out, allowing the hotel staff to choose whether or not to grant them entry. While he relented and even complimented her strategizing, Declan and the assistant clerk stared at them, confusion written all over their faces.

The helpful worker gave them gloves from the housecleaners' closet and opened up the room for them, leading the way. The fifth-floor suite, as big as Wes and Minka's house, came complete with its own billiards table and loft. Hamilton was on the run, in style.

The three of them branched out, each strolling through separate rooms, hoping to find something he may have left behind. At first glance, it twinned any other newly vacant suite, with the bed unmade and dirty towels strewn over the bathroom floor. Minka had just begun her search for clues underneath them when the assistant clerk uttered a loud sigh from the bedroom.

Curious, Minka deserted her own task to join her. "Something wrong?"

"Oh, it's just these inconsiderate guests. They lock the safe with their own combination and then forget to leave it open for the next occupant. I'll have to page the janitor."

This turn of fortune excited Minka, making her wonder if anything may have been forgotten in the safe. The custodian told his co-worker he'd make his way up there soon, so Minka didn't go anywhere until he arrived to assist. When the middle-aged balding man entered the room, she held her breath as he twisted the master key to unlock the box.

She restrained herself from lunging for the first glimpse inside, wanting to appear professional. Once the janitor carried a bag of trash out to the hall, she scampered over and swung open the door. At first glance, nothing lay inside, but upon further examination, she caught sight of something in the shadows. She stuck her arm in and grasped a fresh stack of hundred-dollar bills.

"Hey guys, I found quite a souvenir." She'd never held that much cash at one time.

As they joined her, Cael crouched at her side. "I'd say so, except for the fact that they aren't real."

"How can you tell?" Minka wondered aloud. "You haven't even touched them."

"The Treasury ensures that all bills have an unbroken border. The ones on these are sort of warped." He pointed out the flaws. "Plus, the president didn't have a comb-over."

She fingered through the stack. "There's over two grand here. How could he forget this?"

"My guess is that wasn't a lone stash," Declan hypothesized. "He probably thought he had it all and just missed one, being in a hurry and all."

"Which begs the question, 'Why the rush?' He couldn't have guessed we'd show up," Cael said as he stood.

"I'd say it has less to do with us and more to do with his designs," Minka offered. "Maybe he and the Frasiers have plans."

"Whatever the case, we have to contact the Secret Service. Counterfeiting's under their jurisdiction. I'll call Autumn and tell her I'm not going to make it to the other venue. This could take hours."

"Don't do that, man," Declan said. "I can wait for them. She seemed pretty sore when she left."

"Yeah, she did. Thank you, partner."

Because of the breakthrough, Minka had almost forgotten about the awkward way the couple had parted. As she drove him to the banquet hall, he remained silent, but his worry proclaimed itself. She wanted to apologize for her thoughtless comment, but since Rissdale's name had now surfaced in the investigation, she used the opportunity to catch him up on the man's counterfeiting scheme.

At the hall's entrance, Autumn sat alone on a bench. Minka stopped under the car port, not far from her. Cael stepped out but didn't shut the door. "Thanks for waiting, sweetie. Talia inside?"

"No, I took her back to her office and relieved her of her services."

Minka understood her sharp remark, but Cael didn't appear to grasp the real message. "Thank you so much, Autumn. Maybe we can swing the resort if we aren't paying out hundreds by the day to her."

"You don't have to spend another cent, Cael."

"What do you mean?"

"I mean there's no wedding to plan. After today, I realize how low I am on your priority list. I'm ranked below your job, your partner, and most humiliating, your sister-in-law."

Cael's posture stiffened, and he pivoted toward Minka but stopped short of facing her. He seemed to want to avoid manifesting guilt. "That's not true."

Autumn crossed her arms and let out a tsk. "Well, you didn't prove it."

Minka commanded herself not to get involved, but she had to defend him. "Autumn, we didn't intend to intrude. Declan and I were handling it by ourselves."

"Yes, and that's why it hurts so much." She rose and sauntered closer. "Listen, I've accepted from the time we met how close you two were, and I appreciate all you guys have taken on together. That's the reason I've tried so hard to make a good impression. I began to worry, though, that because of your history, she would always win out against me."

"You two aren't rivals," Cael insisted.

"Aren't we? Because when she appeared, I lost you right away. When we were supposed to be celebrating our future, you chose her."

"I chose to protect this city, including you. It's not for Minka."

"Then, you caught whoever you were after?"

Her question received no response.

"That's what I thought." She stormed off to her car.

****

For it being one of the rare nights Caela hadn't woken up, Minka didn't get much rest. Her part in Autumn and Cael's breakup hadn't won her any favor with Wes, who'd accused her of trying to sabotage the couple's relationship. Of course, she denied it, reminding him time and again that their run-in had been a complete and accidental coincidence. In her sleeplessness, though, she realized the ring of truth in his words.

She hadn't liked Autumn from the beginning, so she supposed her lack of care had translated to a lack of respect. She displayed that more than ever when she hadn't persuaded Cael to stay with Autumn and instead, made an insensitive comment. To boot, she'd listened weeks earlier to Josie Walton's account of Hamilton disregarding her in a similar way, which ended their relationship, too.

She cringed over how she'd failed Cael as a friend, in light of all the ways he'd supported her. In fact, he'd saved her relationship with Wes once when they'd broken off their engagement. She reflected on that day in the hospital room seven years prior.

As Cael lay asleep in bed, she was trying to read the novel in her hands but couldn't concentrate. Two weeks had passed since his motorcycle accident, and though he was recovering well, the pain in his broken arm and leg still robbed him of his energy. She didn't normally mind the silence, but on that particular day, she could've used a distraction from her ailing heart.

Ever since the accident, she'd had to spend time with Wes every day. Having broken up the month before, they hadn't spoken a word to each other until he'd called from the hospital when Cael was rushed to the emergency room. Tension lingered between them at first, but slowly they were inching their way back to where they once were. They even had dinner together the previous night, which had stirred up this quandary inside her. No matter what, the universe always seemed to nudge them together, but she couldn't decide if she wanted to concede to its prodding.

She hated this inner conflict. She was a strong person and never wanted to admit to being dependent on someone. After the fight that led to their split, she had no intentions of crawling back to him. Now, though, she was realizing how petty it'd been to break off their engagement over him wanting her to meet his old friends and not understanding her insecurities about how they might treat her because she was deaf.

Cael's condition didn't help matters, either, as his near-death experience had jarred her. His vulnerable state exposed more of the features he shared with Wes, which conjured up the scenario of what would've happened if he were lying in that bed. She couldn't bear the idea of losing him, especially while they weren't on speaking terms.

Nonetheless, she was too stubborn to confess her true feelings. To ensure that her helplessness didn't rat her out, she decided to leave before Wes swung by after work. It was later than she realized, so she'd have to hurry. Thus, she collected her purse and whispered a goodbye to Cael on her way out of the room. Her quick-footedness proved useless, however, when Wes and she almost collided right outside the door.

"Hey, there. What's the rush?"

"Sorry, but I'm late for work."

"You don't have to report for three more hours." Wes had become familiar with the schedule she'd had for the past ten days. She'd switched to nights so she could sit with Cael when everyone else was working.

"I just need some time to rest beforehand, okay?" Minka replied, her manner brisk.

He took a step aside but then must have noticed the tears streaming down her cheeks, because he grasped her arm. "What's the matter?"

His question made her weeping intensify to sobs, making it impossible to answer him. When he wrapped her in his embrace, she couldn't put up any resistance.

"Nothing new happened with Cael, did it?"

"No."

"Then, what's bothering you, honey?" He wouldn't relent, stroking his fingers through her hair.

"We're not together, that's what's bothering me." Her tears dried up and yielded to her wrath. "And yet, you talk to me and look at me just like you are right now…and just like you always have. I can't stand it! I like being angry with you, but I can't when you do this. Plus, it could've been you on that bike, and I couldn't have lived with myself if it had been. Not after I threw away everything we had over a stupid dinner party."

Wes just stared at her for what seemed like an

eternity, appearing baffled by her loving yet disdainful outburst. Just when he opened his mouth to speak, Cael piped up from inside his room.

"You done, Minks?"

"I think so," she told him, snapping out of her fit.

"Then, just kiss her already," he commanded his brother.

****

In the morning, Minka continued to stew over what the future held for Cael and Autumn and how the mess would impact their feelings toward her. In every scenario she pondered, she earned the label of being the bad guy. If they broke up for good, she'd be to blame, but if they didn't, Autumn could force Cael to sever ties with her. She may not even need to coerce him. Her actions could result in him disowning her, putting a permanent strain on his bond with both his brother and niece.

The tragic predictions in Minka's imagination spiraled on and on. After getting Caela dressed, she drummed up a plan she hoped would repair the damage she'd done. She didn't run it by Wes, for fear he'd command her not to get even deeper involved. Her family's future happiness lay at stake, and she owed it to Cael to intercede like he had for her and Wes.

She set out for Autumn's fitness center, arriving early enough to talk before the first class. As she hoisted the stroller out of her trunk, she glanced over at Autumn's car in the gym's parking lot, anxious. This was the first time, she realized, that she'd met with her future sister-in-law without Cael present. Only having been in her company a handful of times, it'd be that much more awkward to approach her, especially given the occasion. She lifted Caela out of her car seat and hoped the little one would act as an icebreaker.

A couple of mothers were already in the studio with their children. Autumn was talking to one when Minka peeped through the glass door, which made her hesitate further. The intimate group was a welcome sight, but it also made her more nervous, since they could've been discussing her at that very moment. Plus, it wouldn't go unnoticed if she confronted the instructor. She took a step back but had to stop when Autumn gazed outside and locked eyes with her.

Minka offered a timid wave and opened the door. Meanwhile, the disgruntled bride-to-be kept a poker face as she ambled toward her. She left no doubt her anger hadn't subsided overnight. "I'm sorry, ma'am, but I have a full class this morning."

"No, you don't, Autumn," the perky young mother beside her corrected. "Daphne cancelled, remember?"

Minka stifled a chuckle.

Autumn squirmed. "Yes, but this is an advanced class, and she won't be able to keep up. Someone else always brings her daughter."

Minka could've proven her athleticism with a number of tactics she'd become skilled in on the force, but she kept to her goal of making peace. "They're all under two. I doubt that I need tae kwon do training."

Autumn gave up the act. "Please, just leave, Minka. You know, like you did with my fiancé yesterday?"

Nearby mothers failed to conceal their shock and suspicion, until Minka nodded. "I deserve that, but I also deserve a chance to apologize. Please, just let me explain."

Autumn glanced at her watch. "My shift doesn't start for another three minutes, but that's all I can give you."

After the nosey moms inched away, Minka began, "I would have never split you and Cael up on purpose. Even so, I'll admit I didn't make any effort to make him stay with you, and believe me, I would've been just as angry in your position.

"In all honesty, I keep denying it to myself, but I can't get used to the fact that I'm not Cael's partner anymore. Because of everything we've been through, he was more than my work partner. Whether Wes and I had a fight or Wes was on the run from the mob, Cael's was always the first face to greet me when I stepped out of the house. There was a time in my life when the world was so cruel to me that I didn't even want to leave home. That's why it meant a lot to be able to start the day with a kind smile like his flashing back at me."

"You mean very much to him, too. I never wanted to wedge you guys apart."

"You didn't. If anyone did, it was this one here." She touched Caela's head. "Someone was bound to sooner or later. That's just the way life works. It's been harder than I expected it'd be to adjust, and I still hadn't when you entered his life. I guess I was just overwhelmed by it all, and I took it out on you. I'm sorry for that, and I would hate to rob Cael of somebody he loves so deeply."

She smiled, clearly touched. "I appreciate that, and you're welcome to stay for class. Maybe afterward, we can take Caela shopping for her flower girl dress."

Minka grinned. "Sounds good to us."

****

After he and Autumn reconciled over the phone, Cael's mood lightened, making it much easier to focus on work. With the exception of his personal drama, the morning dragged on, pretty monotonous. He and Declan had already checked out the license plate number Hamilton had given the hotel, only to find that, like his money, it was fake. Then, they spent the next hour trying to get the Secret Service to collaborate with them on the investigation. According to Declan, the agents who'd responded to their call the night before lived up to their mysterious reputation, refusing to confirm that the money was counterfeit. Hence, they doubted they'd get any better response today, but they had to persist.

Their call was transferred to several different departments, none of which had a human operator. At last, a human voice answered. "Agent Craig Nichols speaking."

Declan rolled his eyes at his partner, indicating this one was the tougher of the two who showed up to the hotel.

Cael hoped he might meet with more cooperation from him than his younger partner had. "Hi, Agent Nichols. This is Detective Cael Avery with Orlando P.D. My partner and I were the ones who reported the fraudulent cash yesterday, and we were just wondering if we might be able to assist in your investigation in some way?"

"Thank you, Detective, but it's in capable hands here. We appreciate your tip and will inform you if we need anything else."

"I understand, sir, but we're on another case, which, we believe, may be connected to the counterfeiting." He gave him a summary of Hamilton's assault and supposed accident. "To that end, we'd be grateful if you could give us updates, particularly about him or a Tad Frasier."

"I'll make a note of that," Nichols said and abruptly hung up.

Not encouraged by the conversation, Cael and Declan crossed off the prospect of combining efforts with them. Instead, they pursued what they could on their own. To start with, they contacted the banks in the area to determine if they'd encountered phony bills, but none had any claims thus far. If Hamilton had been scattering the crummy ones like those in his hotel room, he was choosing the right merchants to con.

Since Hamilton had registered under Rissdale's name, Cael was reminded of Minka's suspicions about them working together. He read through the same developments she had about the scandal, and the similarities between the investigations were undeniable. The biggest difference was the fact that Rissdale's plot had been discovered, and his buddy's hadn't, even though Hamilton had been bold enough to produce larger denominations. Given that the bank that held Stags' accounts didn't have any reports of fraudulent cash, he assumed Hamilton hadn't involved his business to the same degree Rissdale had, which allowed him to take greater risks.

He wondered again where "the dead man walking" had fled so suddenly. If Hamilton had stayed at the hotel since his faked demise, it struck Cael as odd that he'd ditch it right before they scouted out the place for him. Could he have seen Cael from afar as he and Autumn toured the site? Cael doubted it, given they spent most of their time in the events complex. Like Minka, he concluded the runaway wasn't aware of their presence but just had somewhere else to be.

To learn where that was, Cael called the resort to request their surveillance footage of the time period covering his abrupt departure. Able to review the video before the lunch hour, he managed to make out the suspect under a navy hood entering a gray sedan and driving off. The detectives skipped their break to track Hamilton's next movements with the help of Orlando's many traffic cameras. Things seemed promising—until he abandoned his car at a local bus station parking lot.

"Why would a millionaire take a transit bus?" Declan protested.

"To frustrate any cop who's trying to keep up with him, and it's working."

"Let's call the station to ask if there's any record or surveillance of where he stopped. If not, we can at least go there and scope out the car."

Following through on the idea, the detectives learned the company didn't have cameras in most their buses, nor did they take note of where their passengers boarded and departed. That left them with no other choice than Declan's plan B, which they didn't hesitate to initiate. Eating lunch on the way, they were soon standing in front of Hamilton's getaway car—or one of them.

It wasn't as stylish as the car that was involved in the not-so-fatal crash, no doubt to veer attention away from him. Still without firm evidence of his wrongdoing, they couldn't obtain a search warrant, but hopeful Declan tried the handle. To their shock, it was unlocked, allowing them inside. At first glance, it appeared he had a reason to be so trusting, as it contained nothing of value. Upon further investigation of the backseat, though, their persistence proved worthwhile.

Cael untangled the dark jacket from under the driver's seat. Its wrinkles couldn't disguise the blood stains. "I guess he had someone along for the ride."

"Yeah, and I have a hunch who it was."

Cael's eyes caught sight of something else on the floor, so he wedged his arm farther into the cabin. He latched on to a cashier's badge, which bore Jemma's name. "We don't need to rely on our own intuition on this one."

"Apparently, there's no bad blood between them," Declan quipped.

"Or is there?" Cael had to wonder.

****

Minka could barely stay upright by the time she returned home. The aerobics class had been more exerting than she'd imagined, but the dress shopping gave her more of a workout. They'd perused five bridal shops and changed Caela into at least one dress at each, only for Autumn to choose the typical, poufy frock made of scratchy fabric almost any toddler would hate. The exorbitant price didn't help matters, but Autumn's happiness after she and Cael reunited over the phone made it worthwhile. Everyone was forgiven—except, of course, for whoever dressed the grumpy little flower girl on the big day.

Nonetheless, Minka collapsed on the couch after she put Caela down for a nap. Upon tripping over the mess her brother had made while they were gone, however, she was reminded of the case that had started this fiasco. The controversy over the past eighteen hours had wiped her memory clean of the counterfeit bills in Hamilton's hideaway. Staring at the disaster her house had become, she rediscovered her fortitude to hasten this nightmare to its end.

Because the latest developments all pointed back to Steadman Rissdale, she began searching for the most recent news on him. As in every other case, there wasn't much to tell before his trial commenced. She figured the proceedings would answer many of her questions, but Rissdale wouldn't set foot in the courtroom again until summer.

One report stated that he was out on bail, but she didn't believe he was with Hamilton in that hotel. It would've been foolish for him as a felon to leave Canada and then use his own name. Nonetheless, that didn't mean the two weren't in contact. Concerned about what crimes the duo may commit while Hamilton eluded the law, she tapped into her detective skills in an attempt to pluck out a lead that may have been there all along.

Focusing her thoughts on all the information she'd collected about the friendship between Hamilton and Rissdale, she looped back to the very beginning. Rissdale had been there the night Hamilton was attacked at the bowling alley. It still seemed odd to her that two millionaires would choose to catch up at a low-budget bowling alley…unless it wasn't low-budget after all.

Suddenly, the revelation she'd longed for hit her, and she unraveled what they needed to do.

Her fingers speed-typed a message to Cael.

—*Want to go bowling?*—

****

"Please, tell me you're kidding," Cael cried after Minka related her true motive for inviting him.

"It's our best chance at finding answers, especially since you guys couldn't figure out Hamilton's next move."

"We're working on it," he protested. "You could've at least told me this wasn't just an innocent and well-deserved peace offering."

"I already made my peace offering. It cost me over a hundred bucks and a grumpy toddler. Besides, I assumed coming to the scene of Hamilton's assault would be enough of a hint."

He shook his head, and Minka followed his gaze in Autumn's direction. Unaware of her future sister-in-law's schemes, she'd been wearing the same carefree smile all night long. When she rejoined them after her turn, Cael kept up an appearance of enjoying himself, rising to his feet to congratulate her on another mediocre attempt at a strike. Long past her newlywed days, Minka feigned a gag at Wes, who shot back a warning look.

To keep herself out of trouble, she shifted her focus away from the love fest and concentrated on her theory. She took in her surroundings, hoping to find where this typical bowling alley became something more. It wasn't the cleanest place even by bowling alley standards, and the rubbery pizza she'd shared with Wes and Cael didn't let on to stellar cooking, either. She was sure Hamilton and Rissdale had to have convened there for more than bowling.

It'd be easy to imagine an underground operation going in such a dimly lit and loud building, but it featured nothing else to back up her assumption. There were a couple of leagues competing on the opposite side of the alley and a few employees, but none of them seemed suspicious. With her radar on the entrances all evening, she had yet to spot any unscrupulous characters arrive or exit. It appeared to be a normal Friday night of bowling.

Autumn's voice jarred her from her thoughts. "Your turn, Minka."

She recovered, handing Caela off to Wes. As she readied herself to thrust the heavy ball across the floor, she noticed an employee open the door leading to the service room behind the lanes. She glanced over at the other bowlers, who seemed to be having issues with the pins resetting themselves, and she reproved her wild imagination. Just before she released the ball, the worker reemerged, and for an instant, she was sure she beheld Bryant Maxwell in the shadows, exiting through a back door.

"What was that?" Wes echoed her thoughts, but he was referring to her shameful throw. Unlike Cael with Autumn, he didn't reward her lousiness.

"Well, at least we all kissed the gutter once tonight," Cael remarked.

Minka couldn't form a reply, stunned by what she'd just witnessed and deliberating on how to proceed. She could drag Cael outside and pursue Maxwell, but she doubted they'd catch up to him. More than that, she'd ruin a second evening in a row and dismantle the credibility of her apology to Autumn. As much more lay at stake, she didn't dare take the risk.

Thus, she retrieved her bowling ball and finished the frame. She pretended to be disappointed to leave

just one pin standing and swapped off the baby with
Wes as he rose to take his turn. Her daughter had a wet
bottom, which gave Minka an idea.

She excused herself and carried Caela back to the
room of storage lockers but didn't head straight for the
adjoining restroom. A bowler was changing his shoes
when they entered, so Minka bounced her daughter in
her arms, as if trying to keep her occupied. Once alone,
she made her way over to the door in the corner, which
she assumed led to the area behind the lanes. She put
her ear up to it but detected nothing. With curiosity and
adrenaline welling up inside of her, she jiggled the knob
and almost shrieked when the door opened—only to
reveal a maintenance closet behind it.

Her excitement waned, so Minka moseyed toward
the restroom, figuring she'd better just change Caela's
diaper as she'd told her family. Scanning the lockers,
one in particular caught her eye. None of the others
were marked, available to whomever used their own
lock, but this single one seemed to have initials marked
on it. Minka closed in on it to examine it and almost
dropped Caela when the letters *PH* jumped out to her.

Perry Hamilton.

It seemed too good to be true, but given all that had
taken place over the past month, Minka believed this
was the landmine they'd been seeking. She could only
wish her winning streak would continue with the locker
being unlocked, but no one could be so fortunate. She
had to decide yet again whether to seize the opportunity
to crack the case wide open or to keep her relationship
with her in-laws intact.

Cael's arrival gave her another shock. "What are
you doing now, Minks?"

"Why'd you wander back here?"

"Because I reckoned you were up to something. Now, just tell me what it is so we can go back without worrying anybody."

His insight amused her, but she remained focused. "I threw that gutter ball because I caught sight of Bryant Maxwell exiting the alley through the back door. I hoped to sneak a peek into the area, but instead, I encountered this locker."

He ambled over and studied it. "A lot of people have those initials."

"But Hamilton was attacked here, and his employee was lurking around back. The same employee who supposedly bought Robin's watch and who helped the wounded Frasiers off the grid."

"If it is Hamilton's, it doesn't prove anything other than the fact that he frequented the place enough to rent his own locker. However, I agree it's worth some consideration but on my terms. Just follow my lead…after you change Caela's diaper. I can smell her from here."

Minka obeyed his command—as unpleasant as it was—and returned to her family. She expected to spring right into cop mode, so Cael's relaxed posture disappointed her, as he portrayed that nothing was afoot. Neither Wes nor Autumn seemed aware of their discovery, so she doubted he'd questioned the staff during her short absence. The firm expression he aimed at her, though, told her not to argue with him.

After they'd played two games, everyone agreed to call it a night. Untying her shoelaces, Minka leveled a miffed, sidelong glance at Cael, which he ignored. Rather, he announced that he intended to hitch a ride home with her and Wes, since his apartment was out of Autumn's way. His fiancée protested a bit, voicing her desire for some time alone with him, but she acquiesced in the end. Eager to execute whatever he was planning, Minka's mood turned around, as she wanted to leap with glee.

Cael escorted Autumn to her car and gave her a proper goodbye, before he retraced his steps into the alley and approached the cashier's desk. Minka stood by his side. The worker didn't notice them, preoccupied with disinfecting shoes.

"If I could just have a moment of your time, miss," he asked. "I'm with the police department, and I'm working a case that involves one of your regulars. Would you happen to know Perry Hamilton?"

She shook her head. "This is my first week here, so I'm not familiar with our patrons yet. I'm sorry."

"Would you be able to find out if he has a rented locker?" Minka beat Cael to the punch.

"I don't think so. I wasn't given any information like that."

"Is your manager around?"

"No, he just clocked out."

Cael tapped his fingertips on the counter and blankly stared at Minka.

She, too, was perplexed but decided to take a risk. "Can I ask what the purpose is for the room in the back? The one across from the rear of the alley?"

"I've never been in there, but I'm pretty sure it's just for storage."

"Could we take a gander?" Cael requested.

The young lady obliged, grabbing her keys and leading them back. The narrow hall they entered wasn't wide enough for them to stride side-by-side, so Cael and Minka gave her space as she unlocked the door. She hesitated after she opened it, mounting Minka's intrigue.

Her eyes grew to the size of saucers. "I am so getting fired."

Cael and Minka slipped in to join her. They, too, stood astounded at the major counterfeiting scheme surrounding them. Printers filled the room, accompanied by stacks of fake bills.

"The world's first multimillion dollar storage room," Minka remarked.

Chapter Ten

Declan arrived shortly before the CSU and Secret Service agents. Soon, the bowling alley transformed into a crime scene once again. Since they no longer needed to take Cael home, Wes suggested they leave, and Minka could sense his, Cael's, and Declan's surprise when she didn't protest. No doubt relieved, they didn't question it, but on the drive home, her impish husband slid his eyes over to her in a considering fashion.

"I would've guessed you'd want to stay with them a little longer."

"Well, I'm sure they can manage. I need to put Caela to bed, anyway." She tried to sound mature and logical, before admitting the truth. "Plus, I planted a bug on Cael when I hugged him."

"A bug? Are you kidding, Minka? When and how did you get your hands on one of those?"

"Back in my patrol days." Her confession elicited utter shock to overtake his face, and she struggled to stifle her laughter. "This guy was trying to sell Gus some new security gadgets for the force, but being the fiscally-minded man that he is, he passed on them. Since I had some mad money and had just started dating this mysterious teacher, I indulged myself."

"Let me get this straight: You've been spying on me for our entire relationship?"

She raised her brow at him, enjoying the conversation to the full. "Do you suppose you would've landed in WITSEC if I had? I just broke it out when my curiosity struck. I had it in your apartment until you proposed and then snuck it in your pocket the night of your bachelor party. There was one time when—"

Wes threw up his hand to stop her there. "Do our marriage a favor and don't go any further."

She rubbed his shoulder. "I just didn't want to lose you, honey. And I can assure you I've never used the surveillance camera I bought…well, at least not on you. I installed it to keep an eye on Robin."

"I can't fault you for that."

After they returned home and she put Caela to bed, she started listening to Cael and Declan. Though half an hour had passed before she turned on her receiver, Minka deduced that the owner of the bowling alley hadn't yet arrived at the makeshift mint. Just as they began to discuss how they'd track him down, from a distance Mario Vega started shouting in Spanish.

Upon entering the room, however, he abruptly switched to English. "What are you doing in here? This is private property!"

Cael's voice remained calm. "Your employee kindly let us in, sir, after a person of interest in Perry Hamilton's assault emerged from this room."

"Like I said back then," Vega maintained. "I don't know anything about that night. I wasn't there, and the surveillance footage is long gone by now. I don't understand why that even matters, with the guy dead and all."

"He may be dead, but this counterfeiting operation in here seems to be alive and strong," Declan retorted.

195

"Tell us, how long have you been printing phony dough?"

"What? I'm no counterfeiter," Vega insisted.

"Tell that to all the printers and ripe cash," Cael replied, making Minka giggle.

"I honestly don't have a clue about this," Vega whined, all innocent. "I rent the room out for extra income and don't intrude in my renters' business."

"Who are your renters, then?" Declan asked.

Vega paused. "I don't have to talk to you."

"No, you don't," Cael admitted. "But you will when we request a warrant to go through your business accounts. If you aren't in charge of this scam, I suggest you start talking so we don't arrest the wrong guy."

Another pause followed before Vega muttered, "The guy's name is Steadman Rissdale."

****

"Man, this guy just won't go away," Wes remarked the next morning when Minka filled him in on the prior night's events.

"Nope. Cael's going to work with the Secret Service on getting ahold of the investigators in Quebec and discuss all of this with them." She told him what the two detectives discussed after they left the bowling alley. "But you didn't hear it from me."

"Your sleuthing ways never cease to frighten me." He kissed her head and grabbed his coffee. "I didn't sleep well because I was too preoccupied with Minka-gate. I keep wondering how much you have on me."

She smiled. "If you play your cards right, you'll never have to find out."

He shook his head just as the door to the garage opened.

"Morning, dude," Wes greeted his brother-in-law.

Robin muttered something under his breath, and Minka surmised it wasn't one of his better days. She hoped her breakfast for him would cheer him up. "I'm making you an omelet sandwich, like the ones Dad used to do on weekends."

Robin narrowed his eyes at her. "What? Why?"

"I just figured you hadn't had one in a while."

"Dad made me a couple when I stayed with them last month."

His lack of appreciation wore her nerves thin. "Maybe Wes or I can eat it, then."

"No, I'll have it," her brother whined. "I just don't understand why you're being so nice all of a sudden."

Minka had been debating whether or not to inform him of the latest breaks in the case, and this presented a prime opportunity. Every lead pointed away from him, making it easier to trust his innocence, but she was still afraid to tell him that. Thankfully, her daughter's cry spared her from having to divulge her secret.

She pointed at the baby monitor. "That's why. Because one day, she'll probably have a younger sibling, and I'd like to have some credibility when I tell her to be a good big sister."

On her way out, Minka caught him snickering again, a sight she couldn't grow tired of, given how rare it was. As difficult as he was to live with, that brief moment eased some of her anxiety. Climbing the stairs, she could only wish that side of him would surface more often.

She picked up her baby and changed her diaper, before she headed back down to finish making breakfast. As her foot hit the last step, the doorbell rang. She opened the door to Cael, and Wes joined them to listen to him recount his night of investigating. They both, of course, anticipated every development he related, but neither let on to that. Still, Wes gave her an occasional glance, his eyes beaming with mischief.

Cael didn't stay long, since he was on his way to the station, and once he left, Robin emerged from the kitchen. "Hamilton was running a counterfeiting operation in the bowling alley?"

"Eavesdropping is rude." Minka's remark prompted her husband to give her a sidelong glance, silently calling out her double standard.

"At least it explains why you're acting so chummy with me—you finally realize I'm innocent."

Minka picked up on his animosity but failed to understand it. "Aren't you glad I do?"

He shrugged. "Sure. I'm just disappointed you needed your 'real brother' to convince you of it."

****

Cael and Declan had made contact with Quebec by midmorning but with few results. Though the detective they spoke to was grateful for the input on their end, he had little to say that would benefit them. They hadn't stumbled across anything related to Hamilton in their investigation, and they'd recovered all the counterfeit bills Rissdale had distributed. Nonetheless, they agreed to stay in touch, but when the conversation ended, Cael and Declan again had to swallow the fact that they were pretty much on their own.

Because of the late hour, they hadn't searched the rest of the bowling alley or the locker Minka had noticed the night before. True, they still couldn't prove whether the *P.H.* stood for Perry Hamilton, but with the emergency warrant the DA had issued in hand, they would soon be able to.

Vega was acting as bartender to the tortured souls who'd already had one too many before one o'clock in the afternoon. Not to the detectives' surprise, he grimaced when they entered the room.

The owner manifested a cocky front around his patrons. "You here for lunch, Detectives? I presumed we settled our business last night."

"We just have a couple of follow-up questions for you, sir," Declan explained.

Cael displayed the document. "It won't take much of your time, especially if you comply with this warrant."

Vega's confidence yielded to his shaken confusion, and he excused himself from his customers. "Another warrant? Didn't you guys already discover what you needed to in the back room?"

"Yes, but we suspect there's more here that's connected to our investigation. We'd like to start with one of your lockers—number fifty-eight, to be exact," Cael stated.

"Those lockers contain my patrons' personal property. As far as I'm concerned, you need to get the renter's permission, not mine."

"They're owned by you and on your property. Besides, a search warrant doesn't ask permission."

With no other choice, Vega grabbed the master key and escorted them into the room. Begrudgingly, he opened the one under suspicion, which held a billiards bag.

Vega grinned. "See? Nothing of interest."

Cael stopped him from shutting it. "Not so fast."

Throwing up his arms in obvious frustration, Vega left the room. Cael put on his gloves and picked up the bag. He sat down on the bench behind him before unzipping it. As in their previous discoveries, he caught sight of more counterfeit bills. Unlike in the safe and the wannabe mint, they were loose rather than in neat stacks. He drew out a few of them and found even more discrepancies on them.

He passed one to Declan to examine the ink blotches and low-quality paper. "Man, these are really botched."

Some were worse than others, but it was clear none of them were the crooks' best work. He dug deeper into the bag, and his hands latched onto a note buried underneath the phonies. The instant he unfolded it, he recognized Hamilton's penmanship.

I think I caught all of them on my part. Took care of firing the kid, too. Hope it wasn't too late for you.

Sorry, bud,

Perry

"Looks like the counterfeiting department is hiring these days," Declan joked.

Still taking it all in, Cael realized there was writing on the other side, too. It was a receipt from a convenience store. He scoured over it for any more hints. Though the list of the items Hamilton purchased yielded no insight into the case, the date in the upper corner gave the detectives a new clue.

Cael rose to his feet. "It's dated two days before he was assaulted."

"This could've been the reason why he was attacked in the first place," Declan said. "Maybe his buddy wasn't as fortunate as he was in recovering his stash and took it out on him."

"That would explain why he left a note. He probably feared what would happen if they met face-to-face."

"Yeah, but even with all of this, it's still—"

"Circumstantial," Cael finished the infamous sentence. "All the more reason to track down who this 'kid' is."

After a moment, Declan took a guess, "Could it have been Frasier? He was Hamilton's nephew."

"I doubt it, since Hamilton trusted him to be a part of his staged accident and gave him a lift afterward."

"How can we conclude it was a well-meaning ride? For that matter, who's to say the accident was truly faked? Maybe Hamilton hadn't taken care of 'the kid' to the extent he wanted to."

Cael recalled his own doubts about Hamilton's motive when they found Jemma's bloody jacket. "If he was responsible for the bad batch of bills, his mistake may have caused Hamilton's beating and ended his relationship with his best friend. It wouldn't be a stretch to imagine his uncle wanting to even the scales."

They'd have to set the possibility aside for the moment and report yet another batch of funny money to the Secret Service. Given the poor appearance of the bills, Agent Nichols didn't drive out but instructed them to secure them at the precinct, where he'd pick them up Monday. After they followed through on that, the detectives returned home frustrated.

Cael was set to take Autumn out to dinner later, so while he waited for her to get off work, he stopped over to Wes and Minka's. Wes was busy doing yard work, and since Minka wasn't in a great mood because of

Robin's behavior, he almost left right away. When she inquired about the case, he decided to relate his aggravation.

She took a moment to process it all once he finished. "Do you really suspect Hamilton caused Jemma to bleed, or could an existing wound have busted open?"

"I can't say. She broke her arm, and the shards from the windshield cut her face. It's likely one of her scrapes or stitches could open if they weren't treating her with proper supplies."

"Considering how hasty Tad was to leave the hospital, I wouldn't imagine he's taking many safety measures," Minka stated.

Cael agreed with her and stood to head out. When his phone began to vibrate, he backed out of the room but stopped when he read the ID. "It's the hospital."

Minka rose from the floor. "No way."

He listened to the nurse's report that Jemma had been transported there after she collapsed at a gas station. He assured her he and his partner would be on the way.

Minka lifted her laundry basket after he hung up. "Maybe you'll finally get some answers. Tell Declan I said hi."

"He's kayaking with friends, so I won't be able to reach him. Would you mind filling in?"

She smiled. "I think Wes could pitch in with the chores."

****

A day earlier, Minka wouldn't have believed Cael would do anything to enable her sleuthing, but here he was, driving her to the hospital. He could've handled the interview without a partner and then been free to go straight to Autumn's afterward, so it touched her that he'd included her. It assured her of how much he cared and that he wasn't harboring a grudge over her insensitivity to his fiancée.

The receptionist gave them Jemma's room number when Cael stated their business, and they navigated through the hallways. When they entered her room, Minka held her breath, hoping another dead end didn't await them.

Cael took the initiative. "How are you doing, Mrs. Frasier?"

She regarded him, appearing confused and somewhat defensive. "Better, thank you."

"That's good to hear. I'm Detective Avery, and my partner and I've been investigating your accident. We didn't have the chance to get your statement before you dashed off the grid."

Jemma's head dropped. "Tad's the one who made us run, and I almost died because of it. I've been bleeding internally, which is why I fainted in the convenience store. It's stopped, but the doctors can't fathom how I lived."

"Is Tad around?" Minka asked, noting his absence.

"No, the jerk apparently bolted when I collapsed. The paramedics didn't even know I was married."

"Why did he run like this?" Cael questioned.

"He wouldn't tell me. He's changed after he started working a side job for his uncle. He wouldn't even say what kind of work he did or why he was fired last month. That's when he really became strange. We were about to move, in fact, when the crash happened."

"Perry Hamilton is Tad's uncle, right?"

Jemma nodded. "We were headed to his house the day of the accident."

Minka detected genuine innocence in her. "Were you aware it was his vehicle that T-boned yours?"

She straightened up in her bed, horror riddling her face. "It was? Is he okay?"

"We were hoping you could tell us that," Cael countered. "He was pronounced dead at the scene, but we have reason to believe that was a hoax. We found your jacket in a car he was driving. Do you recall that?"

"I might remember hearing his voice, but that's it. I've been in and out of consciousness this whole time."

"Any recollection of what he said?" Minka's heart raced inside her chest.

Jemma frowned, until her eyes widened in discovery. "He told Tad he'd ruined everything, and he mentioned some guy named Riss."

****

On the ride back, Minka and Cael discussed their interview with Jemma. Both agreed they were closer to the truth, but they couldn't make it out amidst the questions that surrounded it. Though they assumed Tad had to be the "kid" referenced in Hamilton's note, it wouldn't do them much good until they learned their whereabouts. Jemma may have been their best witness thus far, but her current condition would keep her account from carrying much weight.

"I find it hard to believe she'd been in the dark about her husband's work," Cael said.

"I don't. Mine made enemies with the mob, and he wouldn't have told me if they hadn't tried to kill him."

"When will you let that go?"

"When you both realize what a trauma it was."

Enjoying their natural banter, she was reminded of another aspect of the interview. "I liked how you didn't clarify who your partner was when you spoke to Jemma. It took me back to the old days."

Smiling, Cael peered out the window. "Autumn told me what you said about how it's been rough to adjust to us not working together. It hasn't been easy for me, either. Sure, Dec and I get along well, but it isn't the same. There have been times that something arises, and I expect you to give your unique spin on it from across the desk. When you don't, I miss it."

His confession planted tears in her eyes. "Thanks for telling me that."

"And before I forget—" He plucked out the small microphone from his pocket. "—you don't need to wiretap me to find out information."

She chuckled and took it from him. After the moment passed, the two made mere small talk the rest of the way. Cael didn't stay after he dropped her off, needing to get over to Autumn's. Minka grabbed the mail before she retreated inside, where Robin and Wes sat on the couch watching television together. Their jovial spirit pained her, as their laughter and easy conversation made her wonder if she was the problem in her relationship with her brother.

Repressing her sorrow, she greeted them and sorted the mail on the dinner table. Wes responded as usual, but Robin barely grunted. His chuckles and side remarks ceased, and during the next commercial break, he rose to head back to the garage. His sister followed him and stopped the door he attempted to close in front of her.

"You'd better not be angry with me for hanging out

with Wes. I just figured if you were spending the day with his brother, he might as well spend it with yours."

He continued down the stairs, and Minka remembered his words that morning about Cael being her real brother. They'd bothered her ever since, partly because she recognized there was some truth to them. She had grown to view Cael as more of a brother than she did him, unable to picture letting a week go by without talking to him. With Robin, years had passed without them speaking, and she'd hardly given it a second thought.

She tailed him until he stopped in his place.

"I always wanted to be close to you like I am with Cael. When we were kids, I begged you every day to play or watch a movie with me, but you wouldn't. My whole life, I've questioned what I did to repulse you like that. Was it my deafness? Was it because of your kidnapping? Please, tell me now. I can take it."

Robin kept silent, as if trying to decide whether or not the open opportunity to speak was a ruse. When she stayed and waited for a reply, he conceded. "I don't know what it was…and I'm not just saying that. I guess your deafness played a part in it, since our abilities differed so much. Until your implant was put in, we had to have the closed captioning on the television, and you had to put your hands on the speakers when we listened to music. Back then, all of that bothered me, and maybe I was a little afraid I could lose my hearing, too, since it happened to you."

His sentiments pierced her soul, but she couldn't fault him for them. Still, her self-condemning heart chimed in, "Then, I ended up endangering you during one of the few activities we could enjoy together."

"I've never blamed you for that," he responded without hesitation. "Mom, Dad, and countless therapists have asked me if I did, and I've told every one of them no. That idiot took other kids, and none of their siblings were deaf. He would've found another way to snatch me if he wanted to."

She'd never been willing to accept such reasoning herself. "That was very mature of you to comprehend it like that."

He said nothing more as he sat down on his bed and stared up at the ceiling. "Besides, I always trusted that you would've protected me if you'd been able. That's why I wish you could've trusted me about Hamilton's assault."

Minka pivoted away with tears streaming down her face. "So do I."

****

Once again, a lead—though small—was eclipsed by family drama. After her confrontation with Robin, Minka didn't feel motivated to do much of anything, least of all cook dinner. Seeming to sense that, Wes suggested they order pizza, which she hardly touched. Her brother, on the other hand, showed no lack of appetite, scarfing down five slices.

Besides their brief exchange when he grabbed his dinner, the siblings didn't interact. For her part, Minka continued to struggle with her own insecurities. Though she did her best to shrug off most of her brother's disparaging comments, his disappointment in her lack of trust had stung. His voice was laced with pain, not mere vindictiveness, and his sentiment was one she'd never considered. For the majority of her life, she'd assumed he blamed her for the worst trauma he'd experienced. She'd always begrudged herself, and he had every reason to, as well. The discovery that he didn't should have relieved her of that burden, but instead, it added to her regret. She couldn't help but wonder if their relationship would've been better had they faced those feelings decades earlier.

Their young age hadn't allowed them to, however, so they had to do their best to piece together their relationship now. She couldn't rush it, as they both needed a day or two to let the tensions cool, so she refrained from dwelling on the matter. Instead, she told Wes about the trip to the hospital. As she spoke about Jemma's claim to be unaware of Tad's schemes with Hamilton, she started to mull over the other two wives involved and whether or not they, too, were so fooled.

She retraced her prior research in her mind. Rissdale's exploits allegedly began six years ago, before the Hamiltons split up. If the two were in on it together from the get-go, Loraine might be privy to more than she'd want to divulge. She was sure Rissdale's ex-wife would've been interviewed about her insight into his crimes, but Cael and Declan hadn't, to her knowledge, questioned Loraine since they'd cleared her of assaulting Hamilton. Could she be their untapped source?

On a whim, Minka searched her name again, and her mention in Hamilton's obituary topped the results. Given how firmly she'd denied being related to him over the phone, it struck Minka as odd that she'd accept being associated with him now. Could his supposed death have revived her love for him...or perhaps for his legitimate money?

She read through it in its entirety and noted a few

discrepancies from his true story. His actual last name, for instance, never appeared, even when his father and sister were listed among those who preceded him in death. It didn't contain Tad's, either, but she realized nieces and nephews didn't get recognition in most obits. Still, his ex-wife did…

The final paragraph detailed the funeral arrangements, and uninterested, she almost closed the window, but she stopped herself at the last second. The time since his "death" had dragged on to make it seem like months had elapsed, but the visitation and service, both set for the next day, reminded her it hadn't even been a week. With so much unresolved, the opportunity called out to her. She jotted down the address and times with a smile, never more eager to pay her respects to someone.

****

Wes observed Minka as she touched up her makeup before she left for the funeral home. "What? No black veil?"

"Nah. I didn't wear one to your fake memorial, either."

"You haven't told me one thing about that day that's complimented me."

She snapped shut her eyeshadow case. "Sorry I didn't think to go around and record a montage of heartfelt messages to send to you. I was a little devastated and, oh yeah, pregnant."

"Excuses, excuses."

She stuck her tongue out at him, right as Robin entered the living room. He glanced at her with uncertain eyes, and she suspected hers mirrored them, lacking confidence, too.

"What can I have for lunch?" Robin asked.

"There's plenty of lunch meat in the fridge, and I just bought a new loaf of bread," she informed for both the guys' benefit.

He let out his typical mumble, but to her surprise, he noticed her outfit. "Why are you dressed up?"

She wanted to tell him the truth and show him she hadn't stopped trying to prove his innocence. Again, though, she couldn't predict if her scheme would unlock anything. "I have to go to an engagement."

"With Cael, I bet."

"No, I'm solo today."

His face brightened a little, but he said nothing as he stepped back into the kitchen. Wes winked at her, and she kissed him, grabbing her purse on her way out the door.

The silence in her car triggered doubts about her plan, like it had when she drove to Robin's apartment. She started to wonder if anybody like Maxwell or his colleagues would recognize her, or even if Loraine would peg her voice from the call she'd made. Once she arrived and struggled to secure an empty parking spot, she reasoned no one would pay her special regard.

Strolling inside, she didn't recognize anyone from her visit to Stags or her research. It allayed her worries further, but she also questioned what she could glean from a room of absolute strangers. She cautioned herself against giving up, remembering how much detective work starts without solid evidence.

In an attempt to maintain her low profile, she didn't sign the guest book but veered into the line of mourners who'd already done so. A woman she assumed to be Hamilton's mom stood at the front of it, beside an urn of ashes which probably belonged to a John Doe. With at least ten people in front of her, Minka wouldn't make it up any time soon, but she'd already resolved not to use her real name. After all, the woman wanted to sue Robin and may have learned of their relation from her son.

Her anxiety crept back in the farther the line advanced, so she scanned her surroundings to combat it. The spacious home featured several adjoining rooms to accommodate more guests, but even as busy as it was, just a few people occupied them. One chamber in particular caught her eye, given it held two women viewing the reel of photos that played on a television. Her manners prompted her to avert her eyes out of respect, but her intuition forced her to do a double take, as she recognized one of them.

Loraine Hamilton.

After she confirmed her notion correct, she glanced down, contemplating her strategy. If she left the line and marched right in to join them, she'd draw attention to herself and possibly make them conclude their conversation. With how long the grieving mother was talking to each of her visitors, though, she could be stuck waiting for another twenty minutes. The ladies could wander off or leave by then.

The sight of Hamilton in the pictures reminded her of their one and only meeting, and she groaned inside over his blatant stereotyping. Seconds later, the unpleasant memory inspired her escape plan.

She retrieved her phone and jacked the volume up high. Then, she set the alarm to ring in a minute, allowing her to stash it away before it sounded. When it did, she pretended not to notice it. No one said anything at first, and she struggled to keep a straight face as people began to fidget and peek around their shoulders. At last, the woman behind her tapped her on the shoulder. "Miss, your phone is ringing."

"Oh, no. I'm sorry," she replied in a loud voice and rummaged through her purse in haste. "It's my babysitter. I have to take this."

"Perhaps you'd step outside; I'll save your spot."

Keeping up her act, Minka made like she didn't hear her offer and greeted the fake sitter, as she left the line. She strayed off in the direction of her desired place, eliciting a derogatory comment from the lady about the tactless younger generation. She carried on with the conversation about her son, Cael, and his screen time limit, closing in on her marks. Loraine's attention shifted to her momentarily when she crossed the threshold into the room, so she didn't go in farther.

To give herself a reason to quiet down, she began asking the sitter questions. "What games has he been playing?"

While she listened to the nonexistent response, Minka observed Loraine out of her peripheral. She was stroking her companion's back. "We did all we could."

The woman's French-Canadian accent caused Minka to infer she was Rissdale's former wife. "No, we didn't. We walked away, and worse yet, we took their dirty bribes. If we'd stood up to them and done the right thing, maybe we'd still be married, and Perry would be alive."

"You know how stubborn they both were when we tried to confront them, Beth. Besides, we've helped a lot of people with the money they insisted on giving."

Awestruck by her own fortune, Minka had to

remind herself to say something into the phone to retain her cover and encourage them to continue their confessional. "And has he taken a break since lunch?"

"I just wish Steadman hadn't come across those stupid plates. I was so foolish to suggest we make up the American ones to send you guys," Beth told Loraine.

"You meant it as a joke. They took it too far."

A silence fell between them, during which Minka formulated another inquiry about her son. "Did he eat all his carrots?"

Despite the yards between them, she could make out a tear trickling down Beth's cheek. "Steadman called me from prison after he was arrested. He blamed Perry for everything. You don't suspect he somehow…"

Loraine embraced her. "I think they both met the fate they deserved."

Chapter Eleven

After the women switched topics to a less incriminating one, Minka finished her fake call, telling her sitter she'd hurry right home to discipline her wayward child. Only the woman who'd stood behind her in line observed her leave, a peeved scowl on her face. Minka realized the rudeness of it, but she didn't want to risk Hamilton's mother recognizing her now that she'd netted what she wanted to—and more. Plus, she couldn't imagine that the woman would tip her off about any of her precious son's misdeeds. The whole time she was waiting, the woman's expressions of gratitude for "the wonderful blessing he was" resonated through the building.

The instant she sat down in her car, she grasped her phone to call Cael but stopped short. She assumed he was spending the day with Autumn, and after the mess she'd made that week, she didn't want to cause more trouble. She considered this a serious lead, but in all likelihood, nothing could be done about it. Other than her word, they had no evidence Loraine and Beth were involved, and in fact, she believed they were just bystanders.

Desperate to pass on what she'd learned, she chose to call Gus. Like her and Wes, he and Lola had aged out of the honeymoon phase, so they wouldn't mind their day together being interrupted. When he answered, she briefed him on her sleuthing.

He released a cackle. "I'd say your husband's kooky thinking is finally rubbing off on you."

She couldn't dispute it. "At least it's taken this long. What are your thoughts on Loraine and Beth?"

"Well, it sounds like they genuinely didn't play a part in this. If they had, they could've admitted it between themselves. Of course, they could be charged with aiding and abetting because they didn't report it and took a bribe. Since we don't have any solid evidence, though, we can't get a warrant for their arrests or even to look into their financials. I'll have Cael and Declan make a call to the detectives working on Rissdale's case in Quebec tomorrow. They can share what you heard and ask if Beth has given them any cooperation."

She'd expected his logic, but it still disappointed her that her findings couldn't help them more. "Maybe they could search through Rissdale's financial records and track the bribes he's paid to Beth. If they land that, it would give them reason to question her again. Cael and Declan ought to do the same with Hamilton's."

"That's not bad thinking, Minks."

"Thanks. If nothing else, today gives us the origin story of the whole mess. Two rich guys get their hands on bill plates and use them to get wealthier yet. Go figure."

"And at best, it'll end with them both in prison, living off our money. Figure that." Minka could picture him shaking his head. "I'm surprised you didn't call Cael in the first place."

It wasn't her intent, but her voice devolved into a sarcastic tone. "I almost did, but you know, he's in love right now and needs his day off."

"Yeah, and I gather you've been frequenting the doghouse lately."

"Sure have, with him and Robin both." She proceeded to give him a summary of her recent arguments with her brother.

"Well, I hope this is resolved soon so you can get some relief. But stay out of your brother-in-law's relationship."

"Yes, Lieutenant." She smirked before concluding the call.

She wasn't sure how to obey his command when she found Autumn's hybrid car in her and Wes's driveway. Cael's marching out to greet her didn't comfort her, either.

"I heard about your shenanigans today. You've been hanging out with Wes too much," Cael said.

Minka smiled, tickled her husband kept taking the blame for her wiliness. "Who told you? I just finished talking to Gus."

"Wes did when we arrived. Autumn wanted to talk to you about wedding plans."

His statement complimented her, but she didn't appreciate his accusatory undertone. "I wouldn't have gone if you'd given me a heads-up. I figured you would have all kinds of plans for just the two of you. That's why I called Gus to discuss my lead."

He took her bait. "What lead?"

She squinted toward the garage to make sure the doors were shut, not wanting her brother to overhear her. Even though they were closed, she still took a few steps away and kept her voice down as she recounted what her spying exposed. After he acknowledged the same obstacles Gus had, he gave her a commendatory nudge.

"All in all, I'd call it a payday, Minks." His grin told her the pun was intentional. "The frustrating part is we can't cash it in until we figure out where Hamilton's hiding with his stash."

The caveat had already occurred to Minka, and it deflated her spirits. All of a sudden, she made a connection. "When he booked the hotel room after his 'fatal' accident, whose name did he use?"

"Rissdale's."

"Why change his M.O., then? Wouldn't it make sense for him to use it wherever he goes?"

Cael tucked his hands in his pockets, his skepticism clear. "Not if he doesn't want to leave a trail. When you have that kind of money, you can use whatever name you want. I'd hope he'd have some originality in him."

"He must. It takes a creative mind to convert a storage room in a dirty bowling alley into a business opportunity."

****

Cael's thoughts remained on Minka's break in the investigation throughout his and Autumn's visit. As a law enforcer, it frustrated him to learn Rissdale and Hamilton's exes were across town, grieving a criminal's supposed death, when they could've prevented all this simply by speaking up. He'd witnessed it unfold many times before, but regardless, he always failed to understand why someone would ignore the consequences of keeping silent.

Despite his bafflement, it delighted him that Minka and Autumn interacted better than they ever had. His fiancée had put together a three-inch binder full of fabric swatches for the bridesmaids' dresses, which he feared would garner countless sarcastic remarks from Minka. To his satisfaction, his sister-in-law studied each one with respect and offered kind suggestions.

After they'd leafed through half of the samples, Cael could tell they wouldn't be leaving for at least another hour, so he helped himself to a drink. He was twisting off the cap of a bottle of beer when Robin stepped into the house from the garage. He stood in place the instant he spotted Cael.

"Hey, man," Cael greeted him.

"What are you doing here?"

"My fiancée wanted to run some of our wedding plans by Minka, so at present, I'm on a break to recapture some of my masculinity."

Robin's lips creased upward, but he didn't say a word.

Sensing that he wasn't wanted, Cael figured he'd better take his leave and let Robin retrieve whatever snack he was after. "I guess I should get back in there."

Robin stayed put when he started to swing open the door but suddenly stopped him. "Why do you two get along so well?"

Cael didn't foresee the personal question. "What's that?"

"I mean, sure, you were partners, but what's so special about Minka? Don't you ever get tired of her?"

Cael grinned. "We've had our moments. Everyone does. For the most part, I guess our personalities are just a good match. No rhyme or reason."

Robin didn't hide his sorrow. "Then, I guess ours just aren't."

Picking up on the siblings' woes, Cael tried to help

without being too obvious. "Something I've always appreciated about your sister is her drive. Whatever she's doing, she goes at it with more dedication than most people will ever muster. That's why she's succeeded so much in her life. It's even the reason we've managed to make this much headway in our investigation into Hamilton."

"She's still helping you guys?"

"Night and day. She nearly broke up my engagement with that no-quit attitude of hers. She's just never been convinced you were guilty, and it's a good thing because we've stumbled across a lot we wouldn't have otherwise."

His face lit up but not for very long. "I take it you must not have found enough to take this ankle monitor off me."

"Not quite yet." Cael winked and left the room, unable to reveal any more.

****

Cael and Declan started the week with a call to the Canadian detectives to consult with them about the admissions Loraine and Beth had made. They reported that Beth hadn't given them any more cooperation than Loraine offered, playing naïve to her ex-husband's illegal side business. She'd simply stated that if he was bold enough to cheat on his wife, it wasn't a surprise he'd cheat on his company, too.

The four detectives parted with the same resolve to probe through the men's financials in an effort to trace their hush money payments, like Minka suggested to Gus. Cael and Declan didn't find out what success the other partners had, but they only unearthed Hamilton's donations to Loraine's charity. They suspected that was his way of buying her silence, but couldn't prove it.

Right when they began to despair, the forensics department did them the favor of calling them to report their findings from the counterfeiting room before they contacted Agent Nichols. They'd detected three sets of fingerprints—that of Hamilton, Frasier, and Maxwell. They may not have a pulse on where the uncle and nephew were, but they could now obtain a warrant for Bryant Maxwell's arrest.

The accountant was detained in the middle of his day at Stags and of course, refused to talk until accompanied by his lawyer, Chet Jenkins. Because of the attorney's reputation, they didn't anticipate the interview would be easy. In the world of crime, interrogations weren't always two-sided conversations.

For emphasis and intimidation, the detectives carried in pictures from the room and displayed them in front of Maxwell. Both he and his representative stayed stone-faced while being shown the photos of the bills and printers. To Cael, that was a challenge to persuade them to crack.

"This is quite the operation, wouldn't you say?" he prodded. "And rumor has it you had your hands all over it, Mr. Maxwell."

"Just because his fingerprints are there doesn't mean he was involved in producing the money," Jenkins defended his client.

Declan didn't take any time to contemplate a follow-up. "But it means he was aware of it. Since he didn't report it, he's liable to be charged with aiding and abetting. Now, if you can prove otherwise, we suggest you do so."

They exchanged a frown Cael had observed before,

one that meant Jenkins was aware Maxwell's hands weren't all that clean.

Cael leaned back in his chair. "As it stands, we can charge you with criminal intent, at least. We can't speak for our friends at the Secret Service, though. I don't imagine they'll take it too lightly."

"Who's to say this wasn't a joke?" Maxwell remarked.

"The people we've found around town who've received fraudulent bills matching the ones made here aren't laughing," Declan retorted. "We might let you go, but they could still press charges."

His threat visibly dampened the men's conviction, and to the detectives' surprise, Jenkins inquired, "Is a deal in the offing?"

"We could put in a good word for him, contingent on what he has to say."

The lawyer started to demand a firmer assurance, but his client interrupted him. "I've had suspicions about my boss, but I didn't learn the specifics of what was going on until last week. I've noticed an occasional discrepancy in the accounts through the years and have approached him about them. He always had an excuse, and although some were hard to believe, I didn't press the issue because I needed the job. That said, I was disturbed when, every time I confronted him, an unexpected bonus showed up in my paycheck afterward.

"My silence also earned me more responsibilities, but even the errands I often ran for him became puzzling. He'd ask me to drop off boxes but wouldn't say what was in them. Or, more often, he'd send me to pick up his nephew from work or home, so I wasn't surprised to get a text from Tad last week for a lift. I couldn't believe how bad they looked, especially the wife, and didn't understand why they weren't staying in the hospital. Then, he told me he'd helped Perry stage his death but that he was upset they'd been admitted. They'd planned to all go off the grid."

"Where did you take him?" Cael asked.

"To the bowling alley, where I discovered the printers. Tad wanted some extra 'cash' to take with him. I was appalled."

"Not appalled enough to report it," he reminded him.

Maxwell's eyes dropped. "After that, I took them to a dumpy hotel outside of town, and we haven't been in touch since. I'm sorry, detectives. I've avoided questioning Hamilton for so long that it's become my standard. The advantages I've received in return have made it easy to rationalize away my frequent misgivings."

Cael accepted his reasoning but, of course, didn't condone it. "You were spotted at the alley last Friday night. Why did you return?"

"Perry called and asked me to meet him there. Tad told him he looped me in on their schemes, so he offered me a share in their profits in exchange for my silence. I wouldn't accept it…but my loyalty to him still restrained me from speaking up. I just figured with him gone, the company would recover from the marks he made on its finances, and there was no need to blacken his name now."

The misplaced allegiance baffled Cael, but he didn't waste time criticizing it. "A while back, we heard you bought a pocket watch from Robin Parker. We even have a witness who says you paid him to claim to have recovered it from the scene of your boss's assault. Can you enlighten us on that?"

"Maybe after we hammer out an immunity deal," Jenkins intercepted the question and concluded the interrogation.

****

Minka negotiated her way through the front door, despite having Caela in one arm and a bag of groceries in the other. Once inside, she put her daughter down on her play mat before dropping off the bag in the kitchen. By the time she relayed out for the rest, Caela was already lying down, asleep, tuckered out from her active morning.

Before they'd gone shopping, she visited Lola, with her in need of a friend and Caela in need of a playmate. They'd all enjoyed the hour, since the kids didn't have playdates with the frequency their mothers had first intended. When they were infants, it was easy to imagine getting them together on a regular basis, but the daily demands of life tended to limit their stopovers.

The time there freed Minka to be able to chat without wondering if her brother would interrupt. Even so, he dominated the subject of their conversation. Through it all, Lola kept reassuring her that she'd done the best she could for Robin and that, if in the same predicament, she couldn't have managed the way Minka had.

She agreed with what Lola had expressed that morning, that Robin's apathy also contributed to their troubles, but she still wished she'd taken the lead. She debated apologizing to him for it but feared it would just make him less motivated to do his share to improve their relationship. Every time someone else took responsibility for a matter, he deemed himself innocent and hid from his own failings.

She was pondering the conundrum as she fetched the last bag out of her car, and the sound of the opening garage door alarmed her. When her brother appeared behind it, she struggled not to display her guilt on her face due to her conversation with Lola along with her current thoughts. Once she surveyed the inside, her astonishment triumphed over her shame. Last time she talked to him in there, she wouldn't have even stored a dead body in it, but now, it was almost cleaner than when he'd taken it over.

"Well, this is an unexpected sight."

He continued with his dusting. "There's a domestic side in all of us if we search hard enough for it."

"Yours must've been hidden under one of your piles of junk," she teased.

"Yeah, well, I figured I'd better pick up a few things, in case Cael can prove that I'm innocent and get me out of here."

"If you keep this up, I may just want you to stay and clean the rest of the house."

His glower at her showed he wouldn't be a willing participant, but he still offered her a hand. "Do you need some help carrying that?"

"No, it's my last one, but I'd better get it in the freezer. It's peanut butter ice cream. Would you like a bowl after you finish?"

"Sure. Thanks," he replied.

A sudden sense of ease fell upon her, prompting her to take a step forward. "Mind if I cut through? It'd save me some hassle and the risk of waking Caela."

He motioned for her to enter. As she grabbed the doorknob, he admitted to her, "I talked to Cael yesterday. I guess I understand why you like him so much."

She smiled at him. "Yeah, but he'll never be my real brother."

His face remained to the back wall, but she snuck a glimpse of his grin. While she put away her groceries, the air around her seemed to lighten, and so did the tension in her shoulders. Making room for the ice cream in the freezer, she was happy she'd decided to buy Robin's favorite treat, even if neither she nor Wes would eat any. She didn't expect to receive even a word of appreciation, so the fact that he gave her that and a clean garage made her wish she'd bought the gallon tub.

Still, she had to wonder the reason for the turnaround in his attitude. She suspected Cael must've said something, but she couldn't imagine what would've triggered this kind of transformation. As loving and patient as her parents were, their counsel rarely stirred him to change his ways, least of all when it concerned cleaning. Whatever he'd shared with him clearly touched his heart.

She wanted nothing more than to call Cael and ask, but she restrained herself. He'd be speaking with Quebec and handling any possible leads on that or other cases, so she couldn't trouble him for a trivial matter like this. Nonetheless, she couldn't resist the impulse when he called her half an hour later.

"What did you do to my brother?" she greeted him.

"What do you mean?"

She struggled to find the appropriate words. "He's

acting...nice. He cleaned up the garage and even thanked me for a snack. He said you talked to him. Did you use a new kind of mind-control technique to alter his personality or something?"

Cael chuckled. "I'd say I gave him a new perspective. I couldn't go into details, but I told him how much you've assisted us with the investigation."

She smiled. "Thank you. It's made a huge difference."

"Well, I guess I've developed a skill in reasoning with Parkers," he playfully boasted. "I'm glad you two are on better terms, but I wanted to update you on the case. It's been quite a day over here."

Minka listened as he related his and Declan's conversation with Quebec and the developments with regard Maxwell, who was now in the Secret Service's custody. After his general synopsis concluded, she filled in the gaps.

"Did you mention the pocket watch to Maxwell?" she inquired.

"Of course, but his lawyer wouldn't let him answer the question without a deal in place."

"Rightfully so. He may be able to wiggle him out of the counterfeiting charges, but he'd have much more difficulty if he adds fabrication of evidence. Have you spoken to the D.A.'s office about a deal?"

Cael sighed. "Yes, but unfortunately, they have to follow the Secret Service's lead on it. Even now, they deem an accessory to counterfeiting charge too major to repeal."

Minka frowned, her hope of freeing Robin vanishing away. Maxwell wouldn't dare admit to have planted the watch with all the other implications that hung over him. It didn't have his fingerprints on it, so it was his word against Robin's and Jevon Hinckley's.

Grasping for some trace of promise, she shifted topics. "You don't suppose Tad's still at the hotel?"

"We've determined he isn't. We drove over there, but the manager says he never pays much attention to his customers, unless they give him trouble. He also can't afford surveillance cameras, so we couldn't check that, either. Before we left, we scoped out every room for him, too, but didn't find anything," he reported.

Out of options, Minka breached another subject despite Cael's apathy to it the previous day. "Did you search for any properties listed in Rissdale's name?"

"Nah, but I don't think…"

"I'll do it now," Declan agreed in the background. His fingers typed away. "He bought a condo downtown last year but sold it a few months ago. He also owns a unit of storage lockers on Bruton Boulevard."

"I remember that place. It's been deserted for years." Minka recalled asking someone about it when she and Wes rented their first apartment as newlyweds, but it was already abandoned.

"And yet he just purchased it last summer," Cael reported. "What interest would he have in it?"

"Probably the same interest he had in a spare room of a grungy, old bowling alley," Minka theorized aloud.

****

On their drive to the storage facility, Cael and Declan discussed why a tech mogul like Rissdale would buy such a place. As they speculated, Cael remembered Minka's mention of Rissdale's plans to build a branch for his company in Orlando and voiced that he could've purchased it with that intent. They both reasoned the project would be funded by a business account, and its small size wouldn't accommodate such a facility. When they coasted into the driveway and viewed its lack of amenities, they began to suspect Minka's idea was right. With weeds grown up around its rusted metal siding and a driveway riddled with potholes, the property screamed illegal activity.

"Stop here," Declan instructed once they approached the first building. "That air conditioning unit looks new."

Getting out of the car, the pair trotted over for a closer examination. Sure enough, it was recently installed with a gate around it. Not a single copper fitting had been stolen by scrappers, which would've been a miracle had the unit sat there all along.

"Why invest in a new HVAC system when you're clearly not reopening?" Cael had a theory on the answer to his own question.

Declan pointed to the overhead light. "The electric's hooked up, too."

Both continued to quest out any signs of life before Cael noticed that one of the units' doors was slightly opened and drew Declan's attention to it. Without saying a word in case they weren't alone, the two headed that way. While Declan kept his eyes peeled and his hand on his holster, Cael lifted up the door. Inside were, yet again, stacks of cash, from floor to ceiling.

Just like they'd done in the hotel room and the locker, they each picked up a stack, but this time, no discrepancy tainted them whatsoever. The bills mirrored the ones produced by the Mint's press, sure to go undetected by even the most scrupulous of eyes.

"They didn't waste any time in hiring new help,"

Cael whispered.

"This wasn't just a side job. This was an empire. No wonder Hamilton had no problem leaving Stags. This is what would give him his fortune."

"Wrong, Detective," Hamilton's voice rang from behind him, and a knife was held up to his neck. "It will give me my fortune."

Cael drew his gun, only to end up with a revolver to his neck.

"You two aren't going anywhere until we clear out this loot," Tad Frasier said.

****

The entire hour after she hung up with the guys, Minka waited in anxious suspense about what the two might discover. She pictured the area and calculated that it wouldn't take long for them to scout out the premises if it'd remained the same. Thus, the passing minutes indicated they must've stumbled onto something.

Then again, she realized, maybe they'd had to tend to another case once they finished up there and had forgotten to give her an update. The notion frustrated her, but having experienced the chaos of a detective's day, she understood. Even so, she picked up her phone multiple times to give Cael a quick call, until she decided to text him, instead. He didn't reply, so she tried twice more.

When the two-hour-mark ticked away, she called Gus to discern if he had an inkling of their whereabouts. She was forwarded straight to his voicemail, making her want to scream. Just then, Wes swung open the door and greeted her. She started to fill him in on the latest, but her mind began to devise a plan that she decided to keep to herself. Implicating him would lead to nothing but grief…and probably a decent dose of heckling.

"I have to run an errand with Robin. Would you mind keeping an ear tuned for Caela?"

"Of course not. Did you tell Cael you two are headed out so he won't worry when Robin's monitor alerts them?"

She hid her smile, tickled by the irony of his advice. "Good thinking, honey."

****

"I was just about to dish out my ice cream when you shanghaied me," Robin complained from the passenger seat. "What kind of appointment did you say I have?"

"We're on a rescue mission. Cael and his partner hunted down a lead, and something tells me they met with trouble."

He crossed his arms. "You two telepathically connected, huh?"

"Don't be jealous. I'm sure you don't want to be in my head."

"Why not just let your cop friends take care of this?"

She considered his query for a moment. True, her pride and love of her former career factored into it, but her motive stretched farther than that. "Because all of this hurt you, and I want to carry it through to the end."

Minka could perceive his satisfaction over her resolve and was glad to reaffirm her love for him. She couldn't concentrate on the bonding moment, however, having arrived at their destination. At first glance, the worn-down complex appeared to be just as empty as ever, and her cheeks began to flush at the idea of this dwarfing into a disaster of her own imagination. When she spotted Cael's car, relief washed over her, before a new wave of anxiety followed.

She slowed her speed to a crawl, going around the car while she focused on the building. A second later, she stepped on the brake when she caught a glimpse of a black cargo van. Noting that the back door stood open, she gathered it was being loaded, and she could surmise its contents as soon as the couriers emerged.

"Is that Hamilton?" Robin exclaimed. "I thought he died!"

"Jerks like him never go down that easily." She took off her seatbelt and gripped the door handle. "Now, your ankle monitor should be alerting the police, and they should be headed here within minutes. If I'm not back when they show, send them in my direction, and stay in the car. Understood?"

He nodded, his eyes wide. Drawing her gun from its holster, she leapt out and advanced toward the felons.

"I'm glad you guys worked out your family feud," she remarked once she neared them, weapon in hand. "Although it does make me question your business skills, Mr. Hamilton. I inspected his work and wasn't impressed."

The ex-CEO didn't manifest any fear. "No worries, Detective. That's been resolved."

"The printers were to blame, not me," his nephew added.

"Don't you love nepotism?" Minka stated. "On top of that, I'm sure 'the kid' here has a lot to report to authorities if you decided to terminate his services—

and his share."

The uncle and nephew's matching expression revealed the truth in her assumption.

"Can you really do this without Rissdale? He was the one with the plates."

"Not anymore. Rissdale's better at throwing a punch than he is running a business." Hamilton revealed the identity of his attacker.

"So your best bud's the one who beat you. Why'd you cover for him?"

He held up the stacks in his hand. "Isn't it obvious? Plus, I was happy to get that brother of yours out of my hair."

"And you put him in mine, which gives me a month's worth of reasons to use this, so I suggest you don't give me another. Put down the cash."

Unalarmed, Hamilton kept loading the van while Tad returned to the unit for more, making Minka shoot into the air.

"I won't miss next time," she warned.

Frasier marched out of the unit with Cael and Declan at his side and a gun in his hand. "Are you sure about that? Because neither will I."

"I have the upmost respect for you, Detective, but you have to admit they're the only ones here with jurisdiction, and neither of them is saying anything." Hamilton grinned, pointing at the men's taped mouths.

She lowered her weapon. "You know, you're right. What was I thinking, parading over here without a badge?"

He snickered and carried the last remaining handful of bills into the vehicle. Minka remained in her spot, evoking perplexed expressions in both Cael's and

Declan's eyes. As Hamilton hopped into the vehicle, they made desperate but muffled pleas for her to detain them somehow, until a siren blared through the area. They and the con-artists alike whipped their heads around, stunned, making Minka grin. The squad car soon barreled into view, accompanied by Robin in triumph. His sister was rather perturbed by his defying her orders to stay put, but the bafflement on Hamilton's and Frasier's faces made it worth it.

"Well done, boss," Robin sneered, as the officers arrested Hamilton and his suddenly skittish accomplice.

Once they were being escorted to the car, Minka and Robin sprinted over to untie the ropes around Cael's and Declan's wrists.

Robin beamed at his sister. "Guess I earned my ice cream!"

Epilogue

Seven months later

Minka sat, observing the beautiful wedding reception. After much debate, Cael had talked Autumn into a less elaborate venue than what she'd wanted in the beginning, and they never rehired the bridal consultant. Nonetheless, the park they'd chosen for both the ceremony and reception had served as the perfect backdrop.

Like she'd expected, she and Wes were kept busy chasing Caela from the day's start until twenty minutes ago, when she fell asleep in her father's lap. With the daunting "terrible two's" in sight, the tot had thrown a tantrum during the whole time they were dressing her and styling her hair. In the end, however, she loved prancing around in the gown and wouldn't let Minka change her for the planned festivities.

The tired parents shared a look of agreement about taking their leave, but Cael approached their table and delayed their exit.

He nodded to his niece. "She couldn't take anymore, huh?"

"Nope. At one point, I predicted she would outlast us," Minka replied.

"At least she behaved herself for the ceremony." He gave a gentle stroke to her head, before regarding his sister-in-law. "Do you have one more dance in you?"

She chuckled. "I'm not sure. Do you, Wes?"

Cael took her hand once she offered it and led her onto the dance floor. Her conscience pricked her, considering he hadn't spent much time away from his new wife's side all evening. Autumn allayed her worries, offering a wink from afar that assured her she didn't mind.

"Not many married men have time to pay attention to their sister-in-law," she teased.

"This one does, and he always will." He smiled and paused for a moment. "A few days ago, I was cleaning through my briefcase and found your note."

She didn't have to question which one, remembering when she'd penned it like it was yesterday. It was the day she'd given birth to Caela, soon after she resigned from the force. In it, she expressed how much he meant to her and all that he added to her life as her partner and friend. She'd tucked it into his briefcase when he visited them after they returned home from the hospital. She always wondered why he'd never mentioned it but resisted asking him, afraid it'd made him uncomfortable.

"You didn't clean out your briefcase for almost two years?"

He had to snicker but wouldn't let her change the subject. "No one's ever said words like that about me."

"I was hours away from giving birth and very hormonal," she explained, before finally admitting, "but I meant every one of them."

"And I feel the same way about you. Not Autumn nor our future kids or any partner I have on the force will ever take your place. You've gone from my partner to my sister-in-law, to one of the best friends I could imagine." He kissed her cheek, and a couple of her tears made their escape.

After the first chorus of the ballad, somebody tapped her shoulder. She spun around and found Robin.

He smirked at Cael. "May I?"

She would've once taken it as an affront and sign of his jealousy, but they all enjoyed a better relationship these days. He and she had bonded like never before over the past few months. Of course, it helped that they had some distance between them, with Robin having moved back to his apartment the day after Hamilton's arrest. Aside from that, both had made strides to mend fences and tried not to take each other for granted.

"I figured you'd gone home half an hour ago," she told her brother.

"No, I swiped another piece of cake from the table and had to make a phone call afterward. I have some news."

She braced herself, but his smile gave her hope.

"The police academy I applied to in Tennessee had a cancellation and asked me to take the empty spot. I'm flying there tomorrow so I can start training on Monday."

His sister beamed and hugged him. In all honesty, she wondered whether or not he was up for the challenge, but she couldn't have been prouder. "Are you serious? Robin, that's great!"

"I wanted to share it with you first. You're the biggest reason I decided to join the force."

"Ironically enough, you were mine, too." Minka swallowed the lump in her throat. "I don't think I've ever told you that, have I?"

Robin gave a shrug and smiled. "I guess we're even now."

A word about the author…

Karina Bartow grew up and still lives in Northern Ohio. Though born with Cerebral Palsy, she's never allowed her disability to define her. Rather, she's used her experiences to breathe life into characters who have physical limitations, but like her, are determined not to let them stand in the way of the life they want.

Her debut novel, *Husband in Hiding*, was released in 2015, followed by *Forgetting My Way Back to You* in 2018. She may only be able to type with one hand, but she writes with her whole heart!

http://www.karinabartow.com